Down Solo

Down Solo

Earl Javorsky

THE
STORY PLANT

This is a work of fiction. Names, characters, places, and incidents either are the product of the author's imagination or are used fictitiously. Any resemblance to actual events, locales, organizations, or persons living or dead is entirely coincidental and beyond the intent of either the author or the publisher.

The Story Plant
Studio Digital CT, LLC
P.O. Box 4331
Stamford, CT 06907

Copyright © 2014 by Earl Javorsky
Jacket design by Barbara Aronica Buck

Print ISBN-13: 978-1-61188-176-9
E-book ISBN: 978-1-61188-177-6

Visit our website at www.TheStoryPlant.com

First Story Plant paperback printing: December 2014

Printed in the United States of America

0 9 8 7 6 5 4 3 2 1

To my ever-optimistic champion, Linda

That's not the electric light, my friend,
that's your vision growing dim.

—Leonard Cohen

Chapter 1

They say once a junkie, always a junkie, but this is ridiculous. I haven't been dead more than a few hours and I already need a fix. It doesn't make sense; my blood isn't even circulating, but it's the process I crave—copping, cooking, tying off, finding a vein, the slow, steady pressure of thumb on plunger, and now it's my first order of business.

One of the advantages of being dead is that people don't expect you to get up and walk away. I don't imagine it happens often at the morgue, anyway, or they would take precautions against it. Not that I think I'm the first to remain awake through the entire process of dying, or even of one's own murder, perfectly aware of the bullet smacking into my skull, tunneling through my brain, bouncing off bone, and ricocheting around like a bee in a bottle.

I must have blacked out for a bit after it happened. There was a roaring sound, like a hurricane, that drowned out anything from the outside and made thinking impossible.

When the roaring subsided, I woke up disoriented before I realized where I was: disembodied and looking down at the mess that was once me, lying naked on a gurney. I roamed around the room, light as a whisper, fast as a thought, and then returned to the body. When I got close enough, it pulled me in like an inhalation, and suddenly

I felt the heaviness of physical being again. It took me a while to figure out that I could move my fingers, stretch, sit up, and even see through my own eyes. Running the body was cumbersome, like wearing a gorilla suit.

The clock on the wall says it's four. I assume it's at night since the joint is so dead.

As an experiment, I disengage from the body again. This time, I roam the entire place to check for anyone working the late shift, but no one is around except for a technician in a bathroom stall. I re-enter the body, get off the gurney, and shuffle over to a stainless steel tub with a hose hanging above it. I climb in and turn the water on. Some real shampoo would be nice, but at least there's a dispenser with disinfectant soap. Eventually, I get all the blood out of my hair. The hole in my head is weird and I want to poke around in it, but I have stuff to do so I climb out, dry off with a lab apron, and go looking for a stiff my size that has some clothes I can put on.

So here I am in Doc Martens boots, black Levis, and a white tee shirt. The only six-foot-two male body I could find was a goddamned skinhead with a big Aryan Nations tattoo and huge muscles. I hope *he* doesn't get up and start walking around.

There's a clipboard at the end of my gurney. It has a report on it that says "Unidentified male, COD gunshot wound to head."

I need a plan. I'm jonesing pretty bad, so, bail out of the morgue, score some dope to tide me over, and then on to the next order of business: finding out who killed me. The easiest way to do that, I figure, is to visit everyone I know and see who looks surprised.

It's time to split.

¤ ¤ ¤

Good luck. Nazi-boy's jeans still had a wallet with over forty bucks in it. Not enough for what I need, but enough to get me home. I call a cab from a phone booth on Mission. The cabbie is a small, wiry African man with sharp, chiseled features. He's wearing a red-and-black Rasta tam that bulges in the back like a bag of snakes. A slender gold crucifix dangles from his right ear. The ID on his visor says his name is Daniel; his last name is unpronounceable. When he sees me reading it, Daniel says, "It means 'God is my judge.'"

I say, "My name's Charlie, so who's going to be my judge?"

He looks at me in the rearview mirror and chuckles. "I'll be your judge, Charlie Miner." I may be the dead guy, but this hack is starting to creep me out. I don't recall mentioning my last name. When we get to my house, he tells me he doesn't need my money and that he'll see me around. He gives me a business card and tells me to call him in the morning. When I get out he says, "You really don't remember me, do you?"

¤ ¤ ¤

It's a decent little house on Beethoven Street, right off Venice Boulevard. I start for the hide-a-key that I keep under the empty planter, but I don't need it: the door is cracked open, the jamb splintered and gone.

I leave my body and roam for a few seconds, all it takes to scout the living room, kitchen, and two bedrooms. When I get back, I find the body collapsed on the doorstep. I can see that this is going to take some practice. I slip back in and pick myself up, then push the door open and take a real look. My living room serves as my office, and someone has gone through my desk in a hurry. My PC is gutted and my laptop gone, along with the stack of recent case files I kept on my desk. The rest of the house is turned upside down. I want to look around some more, but it's six in the morning and I need to go score.

At least the phone line is live. I go through the kitchen to the door that connects to the garage and find my 280Z, keys in the ignition, and my wallet on the passenger seat. Which brings up the obvious questions: Where was I killed? And how did I get there?

I go to my bedroom and grab an Angels cap that I put on sideways, pulling the visor down to cover the bullet hole. I walk back to the kitchen and dial Jimmy Ortiz's number. He answers like he always does, "Sup, man?" Six a.m., six p.m., he doesn't care. And he doesn't sound surprised to hear my voice.

"It's me, Charlie. Can I come over?"

Jimmy lives a few miles west in the Kingswood Arms, a tall domino of an apartment building jutting up over the small boat harbor in Marina Del Rey. He buzzes me in and I take the elevator to his penthouse suite.

You don't see a lot of junkie body builders. Most of them are into steroids, some into speed, but Jimmy is a China-white man, although he looks tanned and healthy.

"Yo, Charlie, howzitgoin' my man?" He puts his huge mitt out and hauls me in with a handshake. We settle at his dining room table, the center of operations, home to his digital scale, three-line telephone, iPhone, video monitor for the hallway outside his apartment, wireless laptop, and other accoutrements of his trade.

Jimmy offers me a glass of Jack Daniels, which I throw down in one swallow. No effect at all. He slides a bindle across the table, along with a new syringe, a spoon, ball of cotton, and a cigarette lighter. I go through my routine, watch the white powder heat up and bubble, suck it up into the syringe through the cotton, push out the air until fluid comes up through the needle, and tie off with some surgical tubing that Jimmy graciously provides. Bang! I slap it in, push the plunger, and wait. Jimmy watches me the whole time, grinning like I'm his kid blowing out birthday candles.

I wait a minute, and when nothing happens Jimmy says, "Jesus, man, you must have missed the vein."

It's useless, but I can't tell him that. Instead, I just say, "Forget about it. Listen, I got a problem."

"A problem? If that hit didn't put you on the floor you need to check into rehab pronto! And hey, bro, you ain't lookin' too good. I gotta worry about you?" Now he's my grandmother too.

I get out my wallet and toss him my last fifty. "You don't know the half of it," I tell him. "Somebody nailed me with a baseball bat while I wasn't looking. There's whole chunks of time in the past few days that I can't remember."

"Do you remember last time you were here?" He slides the money into a leather billfold he once bought at Harrod's. He likes expensive things and doesn't need some goof like me messing things up for him.

I try to remember. It feels like peering into the fog at dusk. I say, "No, man, I can't picture it. I remember watching *True Detective* last night. How dumb is that?"

Jimmy looks at his watch and says, "Well, shit, it's Wednesday morning. You were here last night to cop. Hey, bro, I still got your phone, you left it here. And we met across the street yesterday afternoon. We had drinks and you were with some new chick—she was somethin' else. You gotta remember her, at least." Across the street is the Cheesecake Factory. Jimmy does business there occasionally, especially if I have company that isn't aware of our transactions.

Memory is a funny thing. You can be standing in a hall with a row of locked doors, then you get a key and walk into a fully furnished room that, until then, might as well not have existed.

¤ ¤ ¤

The room, in this case, was my living room/office. I was pretending to work but was really playing online poker when the doorbell rang. I was annoyed until I opened the door and saw the girl standing there.

She was Eurasian—half Irish, half Japanese, I found out later—small but feisty looking, with long black hair and clear hazel eyes. She was stunning, even in jeans and a paint-spattered *Looney Tunes* sweatshirt. Lizard-skin cowboy boots gave her an extra inch and a half, but her attitude put her somewhere around six foot six. She was carrying a Zero Halliburton attaché, which she used as a battering ram to push by me and into my house. Then she sat in the chair across the desk from me and put her boot heels on the copy of the *LA Times* that was next to my computer monitor.

"So you're the famous Charlie Miner."

"Maybe you're looking for Charlie Major."

"Who's that?"

"I don't know, but he might be famous." This was not an auspicious beginning to our relationship.

Chapter 2

W hoa, man, that shit nearly took you out!" Jimmy's leaning across the table, waving his hand in front of my face. "Jesus, Charlie, you looked like a fuckin' dead person."

"I'm okay, Jimmy," I tell him. "I was just remembering something."

"Remembering, shit! You've been sitting there paralyzed with your mouth open for"—he checks his Omega—"forty minutes. Sup with that, man? You remember your whole fuckin' life?"

So maybe I relived ten minutes worth of the past; how to account for the other half hour? Is this going to keep happening to me? It could have been the dope, but I don't think so—not that I'm going to tell that to Jimmy.

"I'm just feeling weird from getting beat on. I probably got a concussion. I'll check it out." I get up to go, stick out my hand, and say, "Thanks, man. You really helped a lot."

Jimmy comes around the table and sticks the mitt out, crushing my hand—I don't feel it, thank God—and says, "What are you gonna do?"

"I don't know. I must have touched a nerve somewhere in one of my cases, but I can't remember shit and whoever attacked me took my laptop and all my hard files. So, hey..." I shrug.

Jimmy stares at his electronic scale as though it has a secret message for him, then looks up and says, "Didn't you tell me once you backed all your shit up on a server somewhere?"

And it happens again. Another door opens, only this time it doesn't take me out of the moment. I just remember clearly how to access the files, password and all.

"Can I use your PC and print some stuff out?"

Jimmy seems flustered, like the idea makes him nervous. "You're not gonna Google any words like C4 or potassium nitrate, are you?"

"No, Jimmy, I wasn't planning on it. Why?"

"You use words like that on the Net and Homeland Security goons'll be crawling up my ass in a New York minute."

I roll my eyes and shake my head. It's not a natural reaction for me, but it seems like something a live person would do. Jimmy taps some keys on the laptop and turns it toward me, browser open and ready to go. I sit back down and Jimmy says, "I'm gonna go lift for a while." He picks up a pair of ninety-pound dumbbells like I pick up a channel changer and goes out to his porch overlooking the marina. I turn around and start to type.

¤ ¤ ¤

When the website asks me for my password, I enter "BINGO" and, bingo, I'm in. There's a selection of folders, including "Current Cases" and "Priors." I open Priors just for a look; there are over fifty entries going years back, and I hope I don't have to go through them all. Current Cases looks more promising, with only five files.

I'm a private investigator of the most boring kind. I work freelance for a handful of insurance companies and attorneys, scrounging for information on fraudulent claims, witness reliability, and the occasional marital infidelity. Nothing to get shot in the head over.

The first file is a non-starter. Old lady suing a nursing home. She says they stole her jewelry. I never even took the case, just promised to look into it as a favor for my ex-wife's mother. I close it and move on.

The second file is labeled, "Sentry/Timmons," Sentry being the insurance company who gave me the case and Timmons being the subject. Eddie Timmons was a construction worker with a job-related injury claim. He was collecting Workman's Comp and suing his contractor for a torn rotator cuff. I think he was a tweaker; he had a crazed and aggressive way of driving that looked like it was chemically induced, and there was a glint of hysteria in the icy Nordic blue of his eyes. I tailed him out to Palos Verdes Cove, videotaped him surfing on a twelve-foot day, and showed it to his employer. The case was completed but hasn't been moved to Priors because I haven't sent the invoice yet.

File number three spins me out for a moment. It's labeled "Divorce" but could just as well be called Failure, Remorse, Despair, or any other pathetic word that's easy to rhyme in a country tune. I know what's in it and my mind floats away.

¤ ¤ ¤

Allison was a sweet girl when we met. Then I happened to her. That's her version of things, anyway. But if you go far enough back, before the divorce, before the drugs, before the disaster we became, you'll find two people in love. Two college students, not ready, but willing to have a baby when it announced itself by giving Alli morning sickness during finals week in our senior year. And now, sixteen years later, our daughter Mindy is the shining star at the center of my otherwise sad little universe.

I try to picture how a life can crumble as completely as mine did, and I get a slideshow of the Miner family devolving to its current state. The early part, the glorious, exhausting stage of new parenthood, that holy state of surrender to what's really important, only serves to remind me of what is now so irrevocably gone. There's a trigger point, somewhere, a rifle shot that caused the avalanche that changed it all, but I can't put a finger on it. But Mindy, with her sly little lopsided smile and her inexplicable faith in me after all my failures, is still a part of my life. Something to work toward.

Something to hope for.

¤ ¤ ¤

My mind snaps back. File number four is a different story. It sings a tune in my head as soon as I read the label: "Tanya Peterson." My cell phone barks like a dog; it's the only ring-tone I can be sure is my own. The display says "Tanya Peterson." I hit a key to connect and she says, "Charlie, where the hell have you been?"

The voice invites the image.

Chapter 3

We stared at each other for a while. Her left boot pointed right at the cards on my screen. My pocket tens had been matched by a pair of sixes on the board and then a ten on the river, and the other players were waiting for me to call the latest bet. There was over three hundred bucks in the pot, and I knew I could have it, but my visitor was far more interesting. Finally, I said, "Excuse me," and leaned forward, put my hand on the mouse, and called and raised twenty.

My visitor said, "Got mail?"

I told her no, I just had to wrap up a case file, and called the re-raise that came back to me. The cards showed: Screamin' Jay had queens full. Oh, well.

I signed out and sat back in my ancient faux-leather Staples office chair. The tilt function tricked me and I almost fell over backward, but caught myself by hooking my foot under my desk.

The best looking woman I'd seen in years was laughing at me now, and I didn't even know her name. I picked up a pen and legal pad and tried to look professional. She stopped laughing but then started again. Finally, she settled down.

"My name is Tanya Peterson."

"Okay." It seemed like she expected me to recognize her name. I didn't, so I waited for the punch line.

"My husband is Mickey Peterson." Now there was a name I knew. Mickey Peterson was a stockbroker who hung out with movie stars and was a big backer of the mayor's re-election campaign.

"Who did you say referred you to me?" Whatever she wanted was going to be out of my league, and I wondered how she'd even gotten my name.

"Alan Hunter suggested you might be able to help me out." She took her boots off my desk and set the Halliburton on her lap. "He said you were discreet and very thorough."

I wrote "A. Hunter" on my pad and considered the possibility. I had done work for his firm, but had never met him and couldn't imagine ever having been a blip on his radar.

I waited. I could have charged her by the hour, but just watching her was its own payoff. She put a boot up on the desk again. Her hand hovered up by her face, as if to wave off an insect, but then jumped to the briefcase as if it had been stung. She had a weird, restless energy that fascinated me, but then I've always gravitated toward the crazy ones.

She opened the case and turned it around. "As you can see," she said, "there's just a bunch of paperwork in here." She grabbed a fistful and waved it in the air, "I need you to keep these safe for me."

"Safe from what?" Babysitting documents sounded like an easy way to make money, but I needed some background.

She replaced the papers and closed the briefcase. Her hand flew up to the corner of her eye—did she have an itch?—but she restrained it. "There are people who would like to see these documents destroyed. Let's just say the truth won't set them free."

Chapter 4

I must have spent too much time on memory lane, because now I'm hearing her on my cell, going "Charlie? Charlie? Charlie, are you there? For Christ's sake, talk to me."

I say to her, "Yeah, sorry, how's it going?"

"'Sorry, how's it going?' Are you fucking kidding me? Where the fuck have you been?"

I didn't realize we were such good friends that she could talk to me like this, but I just say, "Hey, something came up. How can I help you?" I'm pretty sure I'm missing some key information about this call, so playing dumb is the best fallback strategy I've got.

"Charlie, you're sounding really weird. I don't know what's wrong with you, but we need a Plan B."

I don't know what to say, since I don't remember what plan A was. It clearly didn't go well, I'm pretty sure of that.

"Charlie, what happened to the briefcase? And what did you do to get Jason so crazy?"

I don't remember who Jason is, but the briefcase...the briefcase...

¤ ¤ ¤

Tuesday night at ten-thirty. That was the setup. "At the Cheesecake Factory. Leave Jimmy out of this," she said. "Bring the briefcase. Sit at the table in the far left corner. A guy will come sit with you; have a drink and wait for my call. When I call you and give the go-ahead, give him the brief-case. End of job. Three thousand bucks for a delivery."

And now I remember opening the briefcase earlier that day. The papers turned out to be a geologist's report on a gold mine called Santa Clarita, somewhere near Ensenada. I don't know much about the mining industry, but this report said something about "inferred mineralization" not being substantiated upon further drilling, and that "at current gold prices this project cannot justify additional investment." It was signed by James Caffey, MS. Geol.

Then there was an almost identical document, but this one didn't say anything about not justifying additional investment. Instead, it mentioned "inferred mineralization at $10.6g/ton\ldots$" and "Carlin-type potential." The paper ended with, "The deep exploration potential at Santa Clarita is extremely positive and the chance for deep mineralization is very good. The surface potential, as you know, is without question."

All Szechuan to me, but it struck me as weird that there would be two reports, dated and signed identically, with such radically different conclusions. Tanya Peterson had said something about people who wanted the documents destroyed. I scanned every page and uploaded the images to my online archive, printed two sets of copies and put one set in a file folder on my desk and the second set with the originals in the attaché case and locked it, making sure that my hacking the locks didn't leave any scratches.

¤ ¤ ¤

She's paging me again, "Charlie . . . Hey, Charlie, say something!"

I say, "Look, we should probably meet up, but someone ransacked my house and it's probably not safe there. There's a coffee shop called the Pygmy Up on Lincoln and Superba, let's meet there in half an hour and I'll fill you in."

"You don't have the case, do you?" Her voice is tight, accusatory, and when I don't answer she says, "Why did I trust a two-bit loser like you with something so important?"

I say, "Maybe because Alan Hunter told you to. Now, if you want a Plan B, you're going to have to tell me a lot more about Plan A. And bring me my three grand, I'm pretty sure I earned it."

"I'm not bringing you shit, Charlie. You fucked up big time. I'll see you at the coffee shop with the dumb name." And she hangs up.

I go out to the balcony and tap Jimmy on the shoulder. He's got earbuds in and I can hear Avenged Sevenfold leaking through while he methodically lifts. It's well into morning now and the marina is coming alive. Jimmy finally notices me and puts down the weights. He thumbs off the iPod and says, "Everything copacetic?"

I tell him, "Yeah, I guess. I've got to go meet up with Tanya. Thanks for all your help."

"Tanya, shit, that's her name." He puts out his huge hand to grab mine. "She's fuckin' hot."

I let him maul my hand again. "She's fuckin' trouble, is what she is."

Jimmy says, "Yeah, well, same thing, usually. Am I right?" And he walks me to the door.

Chapter 5

It's a straight shot over Washington Boulevard and then up Lincoln to the coffee bar, but I have to detour to a 7-Eleven near my house. I'm out of cash, my credit cards are maxed, and the Z is thirsty. Last time I ran out of gas it cost me two hundred and forty bucks to collect it from a tow yard. It's a nice little hustle the city's got going.

The 7-Eleven's owner is a guy named Mohamed, but he likes to be called Mo. He's only about five foot eight and weighs maybe one fifty, but he studies Brazilian jujitsu and has plaques all over his little office/storage room attesting to his skill in the martial arts. We've swapped stories over Heinekens in there. I have a few plaques of my own from back in the days before I hurt my back and became a drug idiot.

"Charlie, my friend, how are they hung today?" Mo is Pakistani by way of New York, and he loves American vernacular but always manages to mangle it. "This is early in the day for you." He's always smiling, like a greeter with a lei at the Honolulu airport, but his smile is the real deal, an expression of a natural friendliness and good cheer that I have never experienced myself.

"Hey, Mo." We shake hands. "Listen, I know I'm near my limit, but I'm short and need to put gas in my car so I can go collect some cash."

Mo's smile doesn't diminish by even a millimeter, but his eyes show disappointment. "Charlie, you know my limit is two hundred. You're at one ninety right now, and we had an agreement you would pay it down last week." He shrugs, as if to say, "What can I tell you?"

"Mo, ten bucks, gas. I'm good for it. If I'm late, I'll pay you and I'll mop your damn floors. Anything." I'm groveling, but Mo just shakes his head and rings me up for ten dollars in gas. I feel bad, but not as bad as I would borrowing from Jimmy.

¤ ¤ ¤

The Pygmy Up is a deliberately funky dive that caters to yuppie stoners who get their weed at the dispensary around the corner. It's got thirty different kinds of pies, tarts, and scones, fancy chocolate concoctions, and a decent cup of coffee. I scrounge enough change out of the glove box of my Z to cover myself. This isn't a date and Tanya's not in my good books at the moment.

She's already inside, sitting in an overstuffed armchair with a latte and her attitude. I get a cup of the house blend and sit on the loveseat across from her. There's a cat already on it; he makes a minimum adjustment to accommodate me, stretches, and starts to purr. Tanya checks me out like I'm wearing a clown suit, and I realize I'm still wearing the skinhead's clothes.

"That's kind of an odd look for you, Charlie." She's dressed in jeans again, but this time with a black silk blouse with the top four buttons open. Asians aren't known for having large breasts, so it must be the Irish in her that's stretching the fabric. Different boots, but just as cool and pointy. There's latte foam on her upper lip; it's cute, but then she notices me staring and licks it off, which is even cuter.

She puts down her drink and says, "Okay, look, you tell me what happened and where the hell you've been and I'll fill you in on what was going on."

"Everything?" I check her out; she doesn't even blink.

"Everything."

I know she's lying already. On the other hand, I've got nothing for her, so it's a draw. I wonder what to say next when her cellphone rings. She picks it up and says, "I can't talk now. I'll have more for you soon." It gives me an idea. I tell her to go ahead, talk, and I'll be back in a few.

I get up and walk to the back of the shop to the men's room. The stall is cramped and dark. I latch myself in and try roaming. I watch my body slump forward like a junkie nodding out, then I move through the door and out into the shop to where Tanya's talking on her cell. I catch her saying, "No, he didn't bring the briefcase. What? No, look, you put me onto this clown." She listens for a beat and then says, "Fine. It's got to be one of three things. Either he still has it, or he turned it over to them even though I said not to, or they took it from him." Another beat and she says, "I know it's my fault. I'll handle it." And she clicks the phone shut. Her hand goes to the corner of her eye and I catch it: she grabs a lash with her thumb and forefinger and yanks it out. Then another one.

I go back to the body and move it out of the stall. I look in the mirror and see a guy in a white tee shirt and a baseball cap. I check out the eyes and wonder if anyone's home. By the time I get back to my loveseat, I have a story to tell, from out of nowhere, as if I'd never lost it.

¤ ¤ ¤

I was watching *True Detective* when Tanya called. The show was almost over. She asked me if I was ready; I told her a few minutes. I already had my instructions. I got in my car but it was a warm night so I changed my mind and decided to ride my bike to the Cheesecake. I figured I would go across the street to Jimmy's afterward and celebrate, and I didn't want to drive home loaded. Riding a bike while high is one of life's great pleasures.

I got to the restaurant at 10:25 and went to my designated corner and ordered a drink. There were a few late diners left, and some drinkers at the bar. At 10:30 sharp an unpleasant-looking kid in his early twenties wearing pointy black boots approached and said, "Charlie Miner?" He was about five foot six and made out of wire. Even his hair. There was a movie in the 80s called *Ratboy* and this guy might have had the lead role; the tip of his nose was way closer to me than his eyes were. I gestured for him to sit down.

"Do you have it?" He wasn't giving up a name, but who cared? I pulled the briefcase from under my chair. He asked me to open it. I shrugged and said, "I'm just the delivery boy. And I'm not delivering till I get the okay." That's when my cell barked.

It was Tanya. No hello, just, "Are you sitting with a guy that looks like a weasel?"

"Yep."

"Show him the papers but do not hand them over. He's got the key."

Ratboy handed me the key. I opened the attaché and pulled out the original documents but not the copies. Ratboy reached out as if to take them, but I pulled them back out of his reach and told him, "Nope, not yet."

He said, "Look, it's a no-go until I see the last part of page three of each set.

I separated the sets and showed him what he wanted from across the table. He nodded and pulled out his own cell and made a call. I could hear the ring through my connection with Tanya, then a male voice answering. Ratboy said, "We're good," nodded to the response, and clicked off.

Tanya told me to wait until she called me again. I put the documents back in the attaché and set it by my feet. My back was killing me and I wanted to get the whole thing over with so I could go across the street to Jimmy's, so I ordered a drink. Ratboy had a coke and stared out the window at the boats.

I had another drink, and a third. I asked Ratboy if he was afraid of cats and he ignored me. A man approached. His name was Bobby and he was the restaurant manager. He knew me as a friend of Jimmy's, which made me the friend of a big tipper. He looked at my guest and then said to me, "Mr. Miner, can you come with me please?"

I shrugged my shoulders at Ratboy, who looked startled and punched a speed-dial button on his cell. I scooped up the Halliburton and followed Bobby to his office. He turned to me and said, "Look, this is fairly unusual, but a woman who claims to be a friend of yours and Jimmy's just called and said that you were in an awkward situation and might need a way out." He pointed toward a door that led to the parking lot. I reached for my wallet to cover my drinks but he told me Tanya had already paid with a credit card. Good thing, since I'd left my wallet in my car. I thanked him and went out into the night.

Chapter 6

Tanya watches me as I slide into the loveseat and says, "Charlie, are you okay? I've been worried about you." It's an interesting change in attitude. I wonder how to answer; I'm clearly not okay, although at the moment I'm feeling fairly decent. I tell her I'm fine and she says, "Well...?"

I tell her about meeting Ratboy, showing him the documents, and Bobby helping me get out of the restaurant. I don't mention the copies. She says, "All right, I know all that. What happened next?"

I shake my head and say, "Nope, your turn."

She says, "At least tell me where the case is." I tell her I don't know. She gets up to leave and says, "Well, then our work together is done, isn't it?"

I'm tempted to let her leave. She's hot, but she's trouble and I should have sensed it from the moment she came through my door. There's a bullet in my head and I don't have a dime to show for it and I'm pissed and not about to let it all go, so I say, "What if I could help you get it back?"

She looks down at me like I just told her I could fly, then shakes her head and sits down again, this time next to me on the loveseat. The cat's gone. She puts her hand on my knee and says, "Charlie, I'm sorry. I know I've been an absolute bitch, and you don't deserve it. I'm just under huge pressure and now this whole thing is getting away from me." A tear comes to her eye; she blinks and it runs down her cheek. Amazing.

I put my hand on hers and give it a little squeeze. Two can play this game, or any game for that matter. What I need is the story. I reach out and wipe the tear from her cheek and say, "Okay, geologist's report, from the top."

Her eyes widen. "You looked?"

"I got a glimpse when I showed Ratboy."

"Who?"

"The kid at the restaurant. Looks like Ratboy, from the movie. C'mon, the story."

She withdraws her hand. "I don't see how it will help. What do you want to know for?"

I tell her, "Hey, I'm just a snoop." I've always loved that line.

"Okay, whatever." She pauses, then seems to come to a decision and says, "My husband put his last eight mil into a bogus gold mine." She drains her latte and continues. "He was fully invested in a luxury shopping center in the Valley and the project got upside down after the economy tanked. He had the eight million in cash—it was off the books and didn't show up in the bankruptcy proceedings. Do you know anything about the world of precious metals investments?"

"You mean where telemarketers rip off old people with overpriced coin scams?"

"No, but close. The price of gold has more than tripled in the last ten years. It corrected some but is still strong. There's a bunch of mines, all over the world, that closed down when the price of bullion was too low to support the cost of getting the gold out of the ground. Now that the price is back up, people are taking another look at these properties. Plus, the technology has gotten better for extracting the gold. So, one consequence is that hundreds of fly-by-night companies are buying up drilling rights and then luring investors with promises of the next giant discovery. The pitch is that there's proven gold there that can guarantee at least a double on the investment, but a high probability of finding bigger deposits if they drill deeper." I'm looking out at the window and out of the corner of my eye I see her pluck another lash. I turn back to her and her hand flicks the lash away.

"And people are buying into this?" Here's a scam I haven't come across yet.

"Like crazy. The companies are set up on the Vancouver Exchange. People don't trust stocks any more, and the gold bugs are screaming about the demise of the dollar: that the government is deliberately inflating it in order to pay back China with cheaper money, but that the end result will be a currency with no value and gold at twenty-five hundred an ounce and more."

"Okay, so your husband bought into the story." The cat jumps up on my lap and stands up with his paws on my shoulder. He's sniffing my baseball cap on the bullet-hole side, trying to push his nose under the visor. I push him away but he jumps back up and tries again.

"Cat likes your hat." She seems amused. I'm not. I grab the cat by the nape of his neck and toss him on the floor.

"Yeah, he bought into the story, but it wasn't as crazy as it sounds. Have you ever heard of a guy named Jason Hamel?"

"No, who's that?"

"An interesting character. He has a newsletter that follows gold and silver in general plus a handful of these Vancouver penny stocks. The stuff he's recommended has actually made money, and he has a reputation for being on the ball. Knows his geology, the investment world, and has a good grip on the international scene, the big picture and what it's going to do to the dollar." This chick is way smarter than I thought, but where she's going with this is still a mystery to me.

"So?"

"So he's the guy with the con. He used his own money to buy a property in Mexico, then altered the original geologist's report to make it look like there's enough historic gold—what the previous drill results showed—to make the investment safe, and what they call inferred gold and potential deep tonnage that could make the investment a ten-bagger."

"A ten-bagger?"

"A speculator's home run. Ten bucks for every buck invested. Eight million becomes eighty million. My husband bought it hook, line, and sinker. With him as an investor, Hamel is trying to raise another twelve million. He says twenty is the target for the drill projects and further land acquisition."

"All this on a bogus geologist's report. Aren't there other copies sitting around?" It seems too dumb and simple to me.

"Nope. The previous owners were a private partnership. They had the one report and folded the operation."

"So where are they now?"

"Well, that's the weird thing. They're dead, and one of them was the geologist who drew up the report."

"And you're trying to get your husband's money back." The picture is starting to make sense. I was the delivery boy in a blackmail scheme gone bad.

"He can't do it legally because it's unreported income. Once the investment paid out, he was going to pay the taxes and penalties on the original money, but he can't do that now. And if I expose the scam, Jason can't get the other investors on board."

"So what happened at your end last night?"

"I met Jason at a restaurant in Brentwood. He was supposed to have the money in his car, but then he came up with some bullshit story about needing an extra day to get the money out of some reserve account or something." She looks at me and spreads her hands as if to say, "So there you have it," but I'm confident there are major parts missing.

"So how did you find the original report?"

She smiles and shakes her head and says, "Charlie, you've got the basic story. The details don't matter and I need to hear what happened last night."

At the table next to us, a tall skinny kid dressed in black is moving his head to music only he can hear, drumming the tabletop with his fingers. His head is shaved, except for a thatch of green hair spiking out from the top, and he has a huge beak for a nose. He looks at me and sneers, "What's your fucking problem, dude?"

I tell him, "No problem. About twenty years ago I got drunk and had sex with a parrot. I thought maybe you were my son."

Like Tanya says, there's the basic story, and the details shouldn't matter.

¤ ¤ ¤

The Cheesecake Factory's office door let out into the parking lot right where it butts up to the docks. I took the wooden walkway up about a hundred yards, then crossed the street and doubled back to Jimmy's building. Jimmy buzzed me in and I took the elevator, grateful to have dodged Ratboy and any goons he might have had waiting outside. I figured there had to be backup or Tanya would have just told me to leave.

Jimmy had company. His date was a body builder with breasts that looked like twin howitzer shells. Must have been the Irish in her. He asked her to fix us some drinks and then told me the goods were in the front bathroom. His table was cleared of all drug-related implements and had a vase full of irises instead. The deal when Jimmy has straight company is to act normal, have a drink, visit for a few minutes, use the bathroom on the way out, and go.

"Nice Halliburton." Jimmy likes expensive things. I told him, "Yeah, top secret documents. Secret agents are after me." I was kidding, to cover that I wasn't kidding. It was nice out, so he led us to the balcony and we sat there looking out toward the ocean. We chitchatted for a while. Tanya called and I told her I would call back in a few minutes. I put the phone on the table next to my drink. Jimmy kept looking down at the ground where the parking lot elevator lets out and finally nodded toward a palm at the corner of the parking structure. I looked down and saw Ratboy check his watch and start to move away.

"I hope that's not one of your secret agents." Jimmy thinks the world is full of them. Heroin is probably good medicine for his natural paranoia. I told him I had a bit of a situation and should probably leave.

There was a bindle in the top left drawer in the bathroom. I had just had four drinks and my back was feeling pretty good, so I snorted a third of the powder and folded the rest up for when I got home. On a whim, I took out the geologist reports and put them in a cupboard under the sink, folded into a plush green towel. I left the photocopies in the Halliburton.

This time I headed the opposite direction, north toward Washington Boulevard, and then doubled back to get my bike. I was pretty high when I got to it. The ride home was mostly a dream until I got to my street. It got darker when I turned off Venice Boulevard, and I noticed a silver Mustang, shiny and new, turn just behind me. It caught up and paced me for the length of a few houses and...

And that's all I remember.

¤ ¤ ¤

"What do you mean, that's all you remember? You left the Cheesecake, you went across the street to your friend's and had a drink, you rode your goddamn bike home, and that's all you remember? That's your whole fucking story?" She's just about shouting.

The kid next to us stops his drumming and looks at her and says, "It's as good as your lame story," and then closes his eyes and starts conducting his inner symphony.

I tell her that's when they must have jumped me, whacked me in the head with a bat, and taken the attaché case. That I have strange mental blank spots about the next twenty-four hours. I look at her and spread my hands as if to say, "So there you have it."

She twists the top button of her blouse. I'd like to twist it off, along with the rest of them, but then what could I do? I honestly don't know. She says, "So what do you mean, maybe you can help me get it back?"

I tell her that I switched out the reports and that all the goons got were copies. Her hand flies back to my knee and she says, "You've still got it? Are you kidding me? Let's go get it."

It seems dumb—I was just at Jimmy's—but hey, who knew? What I do know is that nobody wakes Jimmy before two in the afternoon. I tell her it's not that easy and I'll phone her in a few hours, then I get up to leave.

She stands up, hugs me, and says, "I'm sorry I got you into this. And about what I said earlier."

I tell her "No problem," but what I really want now is to get out of here and figure some things out.

Tanya lets me go and takes a step back. She says, "These are really dangerous people. I think they've killed before."

I don't doubt her for a minute. I tell her, "Hey, I'm unkillable."

Chapter 7

I step out into the Venice morning. Traffic is heavy on Lincoln, both ways, and the shops are starting to open. There's not a cloud in the sky, but the scene looks like a charcoal sketch to me. Some people brag about dreaming in color, but I think anyone who dreams in black and white must be in need of some new meds. I watch the traffic light change and the cars start moving. The difference between red and green is subtle when they're both just shades of gray.

I'm in the Z and buckling up when my cell rings. The screen tells me it's my ex-wife. I could ignore it, but instead I answer with one of her favorite lines: "I've got a headache and I'm not in the mood."

She says, "You need to come over here right away." It's 9:00 a.m. and she's slurring her words.

"I don't think so," I tell her. I've seen her benders. She can get crazier than a bag full of rats in a burning meth lab, and I prefer to stay as far away as possible.

There's a click, and my daughter picks up an extension. "Dad, for Christ's sake, get me out of here." She sounds desperate.

Allison screams, "You get off the line right now, you little bitch. Charlie, get your ass over here now and pick up your goddamn drug-addict daughter or I'm sending her to a lockdown in Montana. I've already got the paperwork."

We've been through this before. The out-of-state facilities she's researched are for hard-core addicts and juvenile offenders. Mindy's fifteen and likes to smoke weed. I tell Allison I'm on my way.

Mindy survived our divorce and remained the A student she had always been right up until the end of middle school; then she got an older boyfriend, lost interest in grades, and stopped hanging out with her high-achiever friends. It didn't help that her mother was getting loopier by the week, or that her dad was a drug addict that could only see her on alternate weekends. But our bond has remained intact and she appreciates that I accept her changes.

The 405 north to the Valley isn't as bad as southbound traffic. I get a hint of nostalgia every time I drive out to my old house in Encino, but as I get closer I start to dread the encounter and realize that I can't take Mindy with me. Living with her mom might be hell, but my own house doesn't seem like a sane place to bring a teenager.

I pull into the driveway and there's Mindy standing by the garage crying. I get out and she runs to me. Her hair is wild, her sunglasses skewed, and she has a bruise on her right cheek. I hug her for a moment and then hold her at arm's length. I point to her bruise with my chin and say, "What's that about?"

"Mom's just completely fucking insane," she tells me. The front door flies open and there's Allison, looking splendid in a ratty bathrobe and, for some reason, high heels. She flings a suitcase in the air and we duck; it crashes on the hood of the Z, putting a nice dent in it.

"Next stop Montana," she screams, "'cause you're not gonna learn any fucking respect living at your loser dad's." And she goes in the house and slams the door.

"Sorry, Dad." Mindy picks up her suitcase. I open the rear hatch and she tosses the case in. I guess she's coming with me.

¤ ¤ ¤

We drive in silence for a while. My car is old, but I've got a new sound system with an iPod hookup and I put on John Hiatt singing "Feels Like Rain," followed by Aaron Neville doing the same song.

Mindy says "I don't know which one I like better, but the slide guitar on the second one is way cool." We drive a few more miles in silence.

Finally, Mindy says, "She was trying to quit. She took a thirty-day chip at a meeting."

"Must have been a painful month."

"Yeah," Mindy says. "But she hung in there."

"No," I say. "I mean for you." Allison's one of those drunks who gets even crazier when she stops drinking, and her relapses are inevitably spectacular.

"Yeah, well... Jeez, Dad, what am I gonna do?" I love Mindy with all my heart. Her tattoos, her crazy hair, her sanity and basic good nature, and the way she has never let her mother poison her with resentment toward me. But as to what she should do, I'm clueless.

"Well, it's summer, so we don't have to worry about school for a while. Why don't we just take things one day at a time?" Fake it till you make it.

"I could test out of high school and go to City College if I stayed with you." She's smiling now, sold on her new future, shaking off the drama with her mother, and ready to settle in to her vision of *Life with Dad.* My cold, dead heart threatens to beat all on its own.

"We'll see," I tell her, and I pull into my driveway.

¤ ¤ ¤

We go in through the garage. I had chained the front door from the inside before leaving because the locks were broken. The house looks okay; the mess is the same as when

I left. I show Mindy to the empty second bedroom and leave her to unpack. I go to my desk in the living room and inspect my computer. The hard drive is missing, so I get an old one from my closet and pop it in. I need Internet access.

When I Google "Jason Hamel gold" I get pages of hits, all on websites that, by their names, look dedicated to precious metals. The top listings include: "Returning to the Gold Standard," "Gold is Money," and "Jason Hamel's Bible Prophecy Study on the Pre-Tribulation Rapture." I click on this last one to see if it's the same guy. Sure enough, the site kicks off with this: "The dollar bears the Mark of the Beast. You can convert your abominable paper money into honest money at findgold.com. Look for our 'WORSHIP GOD' 1 troy oz .999 fine rounds. Help your fellow Christians pave the way to return to honest money!"

Old Jason is certainly a man with a mission. I read on about the Mark of the Beast and world government, and how usury and printed money are Tools of Satan to subjugate free men. There's a link to another site, called goldstockreport.com, so I click on that and get to a better-looking web page that seems to be more involved with the here and now. It's got charts of gold and silver bullion performance over the last thirty days, and a list of recommended mining stocks. There's a photo of a smiling, bespectacled man with silver hair and a tie printed with God's hand reaching down from the sky; he's beaming benevolence and Christian certitude. At the bottom is a banner showing silver coins with three crosses on a hill on one side and a monument with the Ten Commandments on the other; it turns out to be a link back to the Bible Prophecy site.

I try Googling "James Caffey geologist" and get a number of hits. Most of them point to a site called *The Motherlode Mining Bulletin*, which displays an "Error—Could Not Locate Remote Server" message. A Yahoo people search does show a James Caffey between West Hollywood and the Miracle Mile, so I jot down the address and phone number. When I search for the *Motherlode Bulletin* I get a few hits that don't point to the defunct site. I click on one that takes me to TheGeoUpdate.com and an article about the shutting down of the *Motherlode* "due to the untimely deaths of both Caffey brothers earlier this summer." I call the listed number for James Caffey.

The line rings three times. Four. Five. Okay, no voice mail. Must be someone old. Now a voice answers. A woman says, "Yes, who is it?" I don't have a plan for this. I never have a plan. I tell her my name is Ron Harris and I'm with *LA City Beat* doing research for an article I'm writing. I have a fake press pass that says I work for *City Beat*. "How can I help you, Mr. Harris? I'm not really involved in public events. What's the article about?"

"I'm doing a profile on a man named Jason Hamel. I understand your husband did some work with him a while back." There's a silence for so long that I finally say, "Hello? Mrs. Caffey?"

She clears her throat, a long phlegmy affair, and says, "Yes. I have a few things to say about Mr. Hamel. I can give you quite a story about him."

I ask if I can come talk to her and when would be convenient. She tells me she's got all the time in the world, but not much left. It's noon and I've still got a few hours before I can go to Jimmy's, so I say, "How about I drive down there now? I'm maybe twenty minutes away."

Mrs. Caffey clears her throat again and tells me, "Fine. It's about time someone showed some interest."

I hear noise from the kitchen, so I go there and find Mindy bending over and looking in my fridge. She glances up at me and says, "Jeez, Dad, you live on beer and taco sauce? This bread looks like a biology experiment." She straightens up and faces me, squints, and moves her head forward as if examining me. "And what's with the clothes? And the sideways baseball cap? You look like a retarded Eminem fan."

I guess it's time to put on some of my own clothes. I tell Mindy to stay home and keep a cell phone with her at all times, and to speed-dial me if anything seems weird.

"What do you mean, 'weird'? And where are you going?"

I tell her I've got some business to take care of and that my house was broken into. I don't want to leave her, but I can't take her with me and don't want to scare her with the whole story. She shakes her head and says, "Fine."

I change into some decent slacks and a dress shirt. I take a light sports jacket along for the interview. I check the side of my head in the mirror. The hole is screaming *Stick a finger in me or cover me up.* The cap stays. On my way out to the garage Mindy says, "Bye Dad. I love you."

All a guy could ever ask for.

Chapter 8

So I lied. With traffic, the Wilshire District is about forty minutes. The radio feeds me a constant stream of crap about the Federal Reserve and China dumping the dollar and a fifteen-year-old pop singer who's suing her parents. Enough already, I'm switching to music. I punch in "Kind of Blue." My dad's road music when I was a kid and we'd drive to Lake Arrowhead. Miles of Miles. I wonder where the old man is. Haven't seen him for years.

I turn off Wilshire and go up Crescent Heights. There's a church on my right. A few more blocks and then left on Fifth. The house is a neat little cottage with leaded windows and brown trim. I ring and wait. And wait.

The door opens and I look down at a tiny woman with close-cropped steel-gray hair. She has an oxygen tank on a strap at her side, with a clear plastic tube coiled once around her neck and then leading to her nose. She says, "Mr. Harris?" and when I nod, she steps back to let me in. She tells me her name is Cynthia Caffey and her friends call her CC, but when I put out my hand she doesn't take it.

The house smells like cigarette smoke, which seems like a bad idea, but I judge no man. Nor widow. We settle at the kitchen table. She offers me lemonade, which I accept. The drink feels like nothing; it just goes down.

¤ ¤ ¤

"You say you work for a local paper." Voice like rusty scissors, then a cough.

I tell her, "Yeah, I'm doing a series of articles on mining investments and kicking it off with Jason Hamel because he seems like such a colorful character."

CC removes the plug from her nostrils and shuffles out of the room. She returns without the oxygen canister and lights a cigarette. I watch the first drag change her. She stares at me and blows a huge plume of smoke out of the side of her mouth and says, "Jason Hamel is no colorful character, he's a murderer. He killed my husband and my brother-in-law and you can print that as your headline."

"Why do you think that?" I jot down "Caffeys murdered?" in the notebook I brought as a prop.

"Because James was terrified of heights and would never have stood on the ledge they say he fell off of. Ridiculous. But try to get the Mexican police to investigate. Bah!" and she turns her head and hacks like a blender full of gravel until it blows over for her and she can take another drag.

"How did his brother die?" I move in my chair and the lemonade sloshes in my stomach. The motion isn't necessary, but the living appear to be, well, animated.

"Just as ridiculous. Barbiturate overdose. Mark never took a drug in his life. Slept like a baby. I knew them both for over forty years. If Mark was suicidal, then I'm a tennis pro. Bullshit!"

"Why would Mr. Hamel want them dead?"

"He had something up his sleeve; I don't know what. They had a business deal, and he had some money invested. Then the deal went south. My house got ransacked while I was at my husband's funeral. I think Jason took all the papers having to do with the Mexico property."

"Are there copies of those papers?" Maybe I wouldn't even have to go to Jimmy's.

"Nope. He got them all. The thing of it is, James and Mark were just about to publish the drilling results. They were very excited." She shakes her head and pulls on her Camel. "You know he's a religious nut, don't you?"

I tell her I've seen his website, but haven't yet met the man himself. She says, "Funny way to write an article, coming to someone as peripheral as me before going to your subject. Who did you say you worked for?"

"*City Beat,*" I tell her. "He seems to have a busy schedule, but I'm pretty sure I'll be interviewing him next." She settles down after this, so I ask, "Did Jason Hamel and your husband have any disagreements that you know of?"

Now she looks amused. "If you mean besides how to run a business venture, yes, they did. James and Mark were members of the Skeptic Society. They were atheists with a capital A and had their own website—besides the mining site—where they debunked everything from Sasquatch to the Virgin Birth. Jason was very offended."

We hang out in silence for a while. It seems like she's out of material for me, and I'm out of questions. At the door, I thank her for her time. She points a finger up at me and says, "You print what I told you. That man is a murderer."

¤ ¤ ¤

In my car, I call Jimmy and leave a message. There are two voicemails from Tanya, plus a text message that says, **Call me NOW.** *Sure thing, lady, I'll jump to it.* I delete them all and head back. As I approach Wilshire, the church catches my eye. The Z makes a turn as if it has a mind of its own and I'm in the church parking lot.

I've never been much of a fan of organized religion. When I was about fourteen I told my mother that I felt closer to God while I was sitting on my surfboard on a freezing day at the beach than sitting in church listening to someone drone on about the Bible. I never had to go to church again. On the other hand, my condition is peculiar and I don't know whom else to talk to.

The church is empty. I look down the aisle at the altar and wait. It's quiet and serene, shafts of sunlight pouring through stained glass in interesting shades of silver. I take a seat in a pew and leave the body. I hover for a second; it looks like it's asleep, not about to keel over, so I roam. I find the priest in his office, sitting at a desk, writing. He stops and looks up, as if he senses me, but then resumes.

I go back to the body and enter, stand it up, make it cough, and wait. The priest comes out through a door to the left of the altar and walks halfway to where I stand. He puts his hand out, palm up, inviting me forward. He's a small man, probably around sixty, Hispanic, with rimless glasses, and dressed in gray slacks and a white shirt with the sleeves rolled back. I guess he wasn't expecting company. When I reach him he gestures for me to sit. I don't know why but I like him already.

"I am Father Tomas. What can I do for you, my son?" The accent is slight, the voice deep for a man his size. He sits next to me and turns to face me.

I don't have a plan, so I'm surprised when my mouth says, "I'm dead."

He says, "We can feel that way at times. Sometimes we are spiritually dead and ready for an awakening. Depression is another matter. Perhaps if we talk we can discern your problem." He gazes at me with affection and concern, and I feel bad. I don't want to disturb his universe, but somebody has to hear it.

So I tell him, "No, Father. There's a bullet in my head and I'm clinically dead. I woke up in a morgue and walked out while no one was looking."

Now he smiles a little, like I'm pulling a fast one on him. I take off my cap and show him the wound. This gets his attention, and he tells me I need immediate medical help.

I show him the report from the morgue. An idea pops into my head. I put the cap back on and say, "Will you try an experiment, just to humor me?" The smile wavers, and he nods slightly. I say, "Go back to your office, lock your door, and write something private on the page under the page you were already writing on. Then come back out here." He nods again, gets up, and walks back to the door he came through earlier.

I leave the body as he's walking away and follow him. He locks the door. I watch him lean over his desk and turn back the page he had been writing on. He looks over his shoulder to make sure I'm not there. He takes a pen from a coffee mug on his desk and writes *Eli, Eli, lama sabach-thani?* and covers the page. Now he takes off his glasses and puts them in the mug along with the pen.

I wait till he returns before entering the body; perhaps he can sense a corpse when he sees one. I watch him watching me, him standing, me seemingly asleep. It's a peaceful scene. I almost hate to ruin it, but I slip in and open my eyes and say, "My God, My God, why hast thou forsaken me?" He blinks, his mouth falls open. I tell him, "Also, you left your glasses in the coffee mug."

I watch him reassemble his composure. He does it from the inside out; he's making new space for something that doesn't fit anything he's ever known. I watch as shock and fear and doubt assert themselves and dissolve, replaced by a widening of the eyes and an acceptance of what I've told him. Wonder, that's what I see.

"To bring someone back from the dead is the province of Christ alone. You have brought me a true miracle."

"I'm not sure I'm back from the dead. I can leave this body, or I can re-enter and make it seem to work. Is that life?"

"It is certainly something new and different, but I'm sure it has a purpose." He sits next to me again and folds his hands together. "Will you pray with me?"

"May I confess first?"

"Yes, of course."

I tell him I've never done this before and don't know the protocol. He tells me, "Say what's on your mind. Say what's in your heart. Unburden yourself, for you are already forgiven."

The words pour out. I am not in charge of this. I might run the body, but I'm not running the mouth; it's on its own. I hear myself say, "My sins of commission are trivial. I have told many untruths. My sins of omission are another matter. Selfishness and sloth. An unwillingness to face conflict. To make commitments. I have failed my daughter. I have medicated pain until I numbed myself to life. I have squandered the gift of living and been useful to no one." I have always known these things, but never articulated them, not even to myself. It's a shabby confession: Charlie Miner, junkie loser. Make that dead junkie loser.

Father Tomas regards me contemplatively; I am his personal miracle. We sit in silence. Now he takes my hand and slides off the bench to a kneeling position, pulling me along with him. We kneel in silence; perhaps I'm supposed to be praying. My eyes are closed. I hear Father Tomas say, "Father, forgive us our sins. May we find peace and purpose in your love. Amen." He gives a slight, affirmative shake to my hand and we stand.

I thank him and turn to leave. I don't know what just happened but I feel something new, a sprig of optimism. Perhaps this is what they call hope. As I walk toward the church doors, I notice a hint of blue and yellow on the floor. I turn and look up at the stained glass.

I walk out into the sunlight. I will the body to move. I will the heart to pump the blood to feed the cells to imitate life.

¤ ¤ ¤

Back in the Z, I crank the ignition and buckle up. I check my cell: four calls and three text messages, all from Tanya. I call Jimmy and leave another message. It's just past three and now I'm worried. Jimmy always calls back.

Traffic's bad. I take Olympic most of the way. My cell rings and I answer it. Tanya screams at me, "Charlie, everything I have is on the line here. You can't just ignore me."

"I'm heading over there right now," I tell her. I turn south on Centinela.

"Over where? I'll meet you there, where is it?" Give me a demanding female voice and my mind switches off. I tell her I have to do this alone or it won't happen, and that I'll call her the second I have it. The reports are in Jimmy's bathroom, and there's nothing I can do until Jimmy lets me in.

Chapter 9

Jimmy's Hummer is in his spot in the underground parking. I slide in next to it and park in his guest spot. I call one more time but get voice mail. When I push his suite number from the panel I get nothing. A resident uses a passkey to open the door to the lobby and doesn't object when I follow her in. We ride up the elevator in silence.

I take the final few floors alone. I take off my baseball cap and check my head in the mirrored wall of the elevator. There's almost enough hair, I decide, to do a combover, so I push a few strands over the hole with my fingers. I guess it's better, but I put the cap back on.

There are only four suites at the top, and Jimmy's is to the left. I've got a bad feeling about this and it gets worse when I see his door, which looks a lot like the front door to my own house, smashed inward and splintered to bits where the locks took the frame with them.

I push the door open and call out to Jimmy. Nothing. I duck into the guest bedroom, which is the first turn off the hall, and into the bathroom. The cupboards are open and the towels are on the floor, but the geologist's reports are still tucked into the green one. I fold them up and put them in my back pocket.

I walk down the hallway and into the dining/living room, which opens to the kitchen on my right. All the cupboards are open—dishes and cereal boxes, vitamin bottles and rolls of paper towels, silverware and placemats—all are scattered across the counters and the floor. Jimmy's workspace, the dining room table, has blood on it. Furniture has been turned over, lamps broken, and there's a huge dent in one of the walls.

I hear a groan from Jimmy's bedroom. He's lying at the foot of his bed, bleeding from his mouth, his nose, his ear, and a hole in his chest. His room looks like a grenade went off in it. I kneel down and say, "Jimmy," and he opens his eyes.

He says, "We've got to get this place cleaned up before the cops come." He sounds as bad as he looks, but he pushes himself up to a sitting position. Now he's using the bed and trying to stand up.

"Jesus, Jimmy, that looks like a bad idea." He lurches to his dresser and opens the top drawer. He pulls out a purple Crown Royal bag and slips it off a 9mm Beretta. He pulls back the slide and checks the chamber, then lays the weapon on the dresser ready to fire. Next he retrieves what looks like a drafting kit, except when he opens it I see three neatly cushioned hypodermic needles and several glass ampules labeled "USP Morphine." Blood leaks from his chest while he loads the syringe.

"Okay, here's what we're gonna do." He doesn't need to tie off; his veins are already enormous. He sticks the needle in and pulls back the slightest bit until a drop of blood swirls into the liquid morphine, then looks up and says, "Gym bag, safe, scale, get the fuck out, in that order, pronto." I watch as he pushes the plunger and empties the syringe. I check his eyes and for a moment there's nobody home, and then Jimmy's back, pulling it together, an act of pure will. He's moving the body. But it's different. Jimmy's damaged, but he's not dead.

There's a third bedroom. Jimmy brings his gun and dope kit. I pick up the gym bag. The safe is in the corner. Jimmy kneels down to open it. Now there are footsteps in the hallway. Jimmy turns, in a crouch, gun up.

There's a crackle of static and a garbled squawk of amplified gibberish and I whisper loud to Jimmy, "Ditch the gun, NOW, ditch the fucking gun." But he doesn't and it's too late and there's a cop at the bedroom door and another one behind him.

"Freeze! Put the weapon down. Put the weapon down." The cop is young, white, the all-American boy, looking smart in his uniform but clearly a first-timer at this kind of action. He's got his own gun out in front of him, pointed at Jimmy's chest. If he sees the hole that's already bleeding there, it's not helping; his hands are shaking, he looks ready to shoot or jump out the window. He moves to his right and his partner comes in gun first and motions for me to get on the floor.

Jimmy looks from one cop to the other, then at his own gun, and says, "Shit," and drops the gun and keels over.

Chapter 10

So now I'm riding a bus. I moved to LA with my family when I was five, and for the next thirty-five years never got on a bus. My choice. This bus is black and white, an LA County Sheriff's bus, and choice isn't in the equation.

After Jimmy dropped the gun, the cops relaxed a bit and handcuffed us. They got paramedics out to handle Jimmy's chest wound and strap him on a gurney, then they took us away separately.

My wrists are chained together, ankles chained together, my shackles chained to the guy next to me, and I'm watching out the window as we roll toward downtown on Highway 10. There's an odor I don't even want to guess about. The bus slows down as the traffic congeals. A convertible comes down the on-ramp and into the lane next to us. The driver is a blond with a ponytail and mirrored shades. She's chewing gum and moving to music that's blasting from the car stereo, one slender arm resting along the back of the passenger seat. She's wearing a skimpy halter top over what's got to be ten thousand dollars' worth of silicone.

The biker-type in the seat ahead of me yells, "Hey, mamacita, you know what I got for you?" He's got long greasy hair and a full beard, and now he's standing with his crotch pressed up to the window, arching his back and flicking his tongue in and out of his open mouth.

"What a fuckin' asshole," I say, to no one in particular.

"S'matter, man, you don't like chicks?" It's the guy I'm manacled to, a heavily muscled Mexican with a pointy little goatee. "'Cause if you don' like chicks, man, you goin' to the right place."

Go fuck yourself is what I want to say, but I stop myself. A series of X's and 0's alternate on the guy's knuckles, and his biceps stretch the sleeves of his tee shirt. I turn my attention out the window to the road below.

The blond looks up at us and waves her fingers. A bubble grows out of her mouth and then pops and disappears. The entire right side of the bus is lined with manacled prisoners staring down at her.

"ALL RIGHT, IN YOUR SEATS!" a sheriff in the front of the bus yells at us from behind a Plexiglas barrier. Traffic loosens up and the convertible shoots ahead of us with a peeling of tires.

There are more lowlifes on the bus than I've ever seen in one place, except maybe Hernando's Bar out in Venice, and they're in top form today. One of them yells out from across the aisle, "Hey sheriff, oink oink, is that a shotgun or are you just happy to see me?" The officer just stands there, stone-faced, staring straight down the aisle.

Now we're past the downtown interchange, heading out into the industrial flatlands, beyond the traffic, picking up speed, hurtling through the crappy landscape on our way to the county jail.

We arrive and they order us out of the bus and into a single-line formation on the tarmac. From there we're marched to the back entrance of the jail building and into a holding cell, where another sheriff orders us to stand in a circle with our backs to the walls. On our way in, a deputy takes off our shackles.

A huge black guard enters with a clipboard in his hands. "All right all you model citizens," he yells. "Listen up. Welcome back, as I'm sure most of you have been here before. If you follow directions, everything will proceed smoothly. If you do not follow directions, you will find yourselves in deeper shit than you are already in. Got it? Good. Now, I want each of you to remove all your clothing and place it in a nice little pile at your feet. NOW."

I start to take off my shirt. They took my watch and wallet, along with my cell phone and keys, when they booked me at the Marina substation. They must have the geologist's reports, too. Tanya's got to be flipping out. I take off my socks and shoes and wait, looking around at the others. The same odor that permeated the bus has followed them into this cell.

"YOU," barks the officer. "Remove your clothes. All of them."

I take off my jeans and undershorts, roll my other things into the jeans, and lay the resulting bundle at my feet like everyone else. They're all finished except for the guy to my right, who's still fooling with the button of his pants. His clothes are filthy, and his face is entirely covered with hair, except for the sunburned nose and cheeks. His wild black eyes stare defiantly at the deputy. The officer glares back, smacking his nightstick into his palm.

A new deputy enters the enclosure, a wiry little guy with big ears and an Adams apple the size of a walnut. He puts on a pair of surgical gloves.

"Listen up!" The big deputy yells. "I want you girls to turn around and face the walls, spread your feet apart, bend over and grab your ankles."

I do as I'm told. It's an interesting view, looking around the room upside down. The skinny cop starts making the rounds.He gets to me and our eyes meet. "What are you lookin' at?" he asks. He pulls on one of the gloves and releases it with a big snapping sound.

I tell him, "Nothing, sir."

"That's good," the skinny cop says, and he goes on to the next guy.

"Hey, Ed, come here and check this out."

The big cop comes over to see what's going on. He looks down at the guy with the hairy face.

"Oh my God, that's shit," he says.

The bearded guy cackles, "What'd you expect, man, ice cream?" and everyone in the room cracks up.

Except for the deputies.

The black cop yells, "SHUT THE FUCK UP. Now, stand up, turn around, and pick up your bundles."

We march single-file out of the cell and into a hallway. About thirty yards down the hall they tell us to stop and line up against the wall. One at a time, we approach a window. I get to it and hand over my bundle to yet another deputy. In exchange he gives me a rolled-up jumpsuit and a white towel.

Now they escort us to a row of showers, columns placed every five feet along a tiled depression. Each column has four showerheads on it and a tray with bits of soap.

The big deputy picks up a black hose that snakes to a metal tank. The hose has a fine spray attachment that blasts a mist of delousing solution at us. Then he barks, "You've got one minute." He turns to the bearded guy and says, "Clean it good, Ice-Cream Ass," and flicks a switch. All the showers turn on at once and there's a mad scrambling for position. I put my new bundle on the floor and head for the only available shower.

I step under the spray and close my eyes and something knocks me up against the wall. I look back at my spot, which is now occupied by the guy with the X's and O's on his knuckles. I move in on the guy and shoulder him out of the position.

"Motherfocker, you want to fock with me?" The guy's face is pocked and he has tattoos all over his arms and chest.

I check him out, naked with his tattoos and his muscles and his little silver earring, and point to his groin. "Hey, check it out, size counts. Bummer for your girlfriend. Give me a fuckin' break." People around us start laughing. I see the big cop coming over, so I turn my back and soap up my armpits. The hissing of the shower stops abruptly, leaving the room in silence except for the dripping of the nozzles and the sound of bare feet padding across the tiles.

I turn around to see the gangbanger up against the wall with the big cop's baton between his shoulder blades. Another deputy comes and takes the guy away. I dry off and put on the jumpsuit. It's too small—the pant legs end at my shins—but it's good to be covered up. We march down the hall to a stairway and deposit our towels in a bin on the way.

We line up at the entrance to a room as big as a basketball court, full of men in jumpsuits. A deputy hands me a new towel and a mat like a gymnastics pad but the size of a single bed. The huge room is filled with steel-framed bunk beds. In the corridors between the closely spaced bunks, inmates are playing cards, gathered in groups, or just sitting and watching the general commotion. I drag my mat around, looking for an empty spot, and notice a small black man with dreadlocks holding a bulging file envelope and chanting, "Ey, mon, condee, smokes, brush ya teeth."

It's Daniel, my taxi driver.

I say, "What are you doing here?"

He grins, beautiful, big white teeth, and says, "You never called me. Looks like you could use some help." No accent at all. He winks.

I say, "Help me find a spot and I'll do business with you later. Maybe in a corner where it's not so noisy, and..."

"And where de brothers don' hang together, is dot what you want to seh?"

"Just keep me away from the gangbangers, that's all."

"Mebbe you want de penthouse suite," the guy says. "Come on."

I follow him to the far corner of the room. It's quieter; the inmates look older and keep to themselves or converse in pairs. A top bunk has no mattress on it. I hoist mine up and position it on the frame.

"Okay, thanks, Daniel. This is good."

Someone from a nearby bunk makes a hand gesture that gets Daniel's attention. As he ambles off to ply his wares, I launch myself up to my new home and fold my towel into a pillow. I nod at my neighbor, a skeletal little Asian man with silver hair flowing to his shoulders, who inclines his head so slightly I'm not even sure it's a response.

There's nothing to do but check out. I feel tired anyway. I lay my head on the makeshift pillow and stare up at the holes in the soundproof tiles above. The general din condenses into a faraway buzz and then gets swallowed by sleep.

I'm deep in a dream when the bunk moves. I was driving a car, but couldn't reach the brake pedal because I was in the back seat, reaching around the driver's side headrest to steer. Through the windshield I could see a thousand brake lights all go on at once. When the bed moves, I open my eyes. Sitting over me, perched right next to my shoulder and looking down at me, is the guy with the tattoos. I prop myself up on my elbows.

"You don' fock with a man like that," the guy says. I wonder if I can get my thumb into the guy's eye socket fast enough, and decide probably not.

Just to mess with him, I say, "If you wanted my shower, you should have asked politely."

"Oh, you gonna be cute with me, huh? Huh? Fockin' ponk. I think you need to learn some respect."

I look up at the guy, his thick arms and his pointy little beard, and say, "Why don't you decide exactly how far you want to go with this, right now, and then go for it?" I sit up, and now I'm facing the guy. We're inches apart. You have to look the really crazy ones right in the eye.

Years ago, some cocaine-crazed giant came up to the table where I was sitting with some friends in a blues club out in the Valley. The guy put the point of a Buck knife to my throat and said, "Put your drink down and your hands on your knees." Instead, I lifted the glass to my mouth and took a swallow. The guy was clearly batshit crazy, looked like he weighed three hundred pounds. "Put your drink down and then put your hands on your knees," the guy repeated, and I took another swig of my JD. After a beat, the guy said, "Hey, man, I thought you were somebody else," and then lumbered away.

The gangbanger's eyes flicker for a moment, then shift to the old Asian man. "What are you lookin' at, faggot?" the guy says. The old man stares impassively and says nothing. With the tattooed guy's hostility deflected for a moment, I feel the heat dissipate. I watch him swagger away as if he's just won a victory. I fade into sleep again.

Chapter 11

In my new dream I'm in a room, the shadows are red, and my pulse in my ears multiplies into drums—congas and bongos and a deep bass that sounds like a whale gulping air. Someone else chimes in with a rattle that snakes its own way through the beat. It's smoky and the room is crowded. I'm sitting across from a thin Hispanic man at the center of the crowd. He's wearing a wrinkled black suit, a narrow tie, and a kufi cap with a mandala pattern. He raises his hand and the drumming stops. The room goes silent.

"We are gathered here tonight to bring our friend Charlie out of the darkness." His voice is a memory, I know it intimately, its deep and precise tone filling the room. A brazier with a small flame sits between us, casting jumpy shadows on the walls; a stream of fragrant but acrid smoke curls to the ceiling.

"We imagine we are human beings, searching for a spiritual experience, but in fact we are spiritual beings having a human experience."

The drumming resumes, quietly, but with a rock-steady pulse. A wiry, dreadlocked man with skin as black as Mindy's fingernail polish steps into the inner circle with us and hands the man a cup. He sips from it and hands it to me. The drums tease their way forward, floating over the beat of the gulping whale, weaving a net that pulls me into the flame, up with the smoke, and through the roof. I hear the man say, "The spirit knows how to leave the body, heal the body..."

And I'm out, floating free, roaming under the dawn sky, unburdened by care or desire. There is a house far below me, the size of a postage stamp, in the middle of a field, cars and trucks parked haphazardly by the entrance. The field is divided neatly into squares, with rows of green divided by shining lines of water. An armadillo scurries out from under a bush; like a hawk, I swoop down to investigate. Its startled face turns up, then left and right. It can't see me, but it curls up into a ball. It knows something is there.

There's a clown standing in the field. I move toward it and see that it's a scarecrow with a red rubber ball for a nose. Its face is covered with bees. Their buzzing gets louder until it becomes a maddening roar and they fly away, leaving, instead of a scarecrow, my face. My body is on a cross, I'm wearing a crown of thorns, and it suddenly sprouts roses in an explosion of red.

Now I'm back in the room, looking down on my body lying flat on the floor. Without a thought, I enter it. My body starts to shake. It has its very own earthquake, and panic overwhelms me. The man with the narrow tie leans over me, mouthing words I can't make out. The pattern on his kufi moves from the center outward like a mad kaleidoscope. His hand shoots out and grabs my wrist. I try to pull away, but I'm paralyzed with dread. I close my eyes. *Help me. Dear God, please help me.*

My arm is being shaken now.

I open my eyes and see Daniel, his hand around my wrist. He grins, big white teeth and clear eyes under the wild dreadlocks. He lets go of my wrist and suddenly grows serious, sniffing the air as if trying to place an odor.

"You," he says, pointing his finger at me, "been back to de room."

"What room?"

"De room in Mexico, mon." Daniel's eyes narrow as he peers up at me.

"What room in Mexico? And how would you know about that?" The guy has to be crazy.

He shakes his head. "You really need to wake up. I bet you never looked at de card I gave you, right?"

He's right. The card is still in my pocket, or in the packet the cops put my stuff in.

He winks and then says, "When you get out of here, you check out what's on dat card, den come find me at Venice Beach, on de boardwalk, and I tell you much more. Right now, I got to go do business." He starts to leave, then turns around.

"Good ting you come back from dat dream." He looks back at me, serious for a moment, then throws back his head and laughs. "You a very lucky mon," he says, and then walks away.

¤ ¤ ¤

A bell clangs and the huge room becomes the scene of a massive clutter of random movement that somehow resolves itself into two neat lines of blue-jumpsuited men. We stand heel to toe facing the doorway to the maze of inner hallways. A deputy gives the signal, and the line I'm in begins to move.

"Shoulders against the walls. Keep your hands at your sides. NO TALKING, ASSHOLE!" A crew-cut deputy with a bright red face and neck approaches the line and thrusts his face up into the face of a muscular black man several places in front of me.

The line stops moving. The deputy's shirt outlines the V-shape from his waist to his armpits and is stretched taut across his back.

"You wanna fuck with me?" The deputy, who's about five foot eight, looks up at the inmate, who stands at about my height of just over six feet. Both men's muscles twitch as they stare at each other. The black man's fingers extend stiffly, as if he's straining to avoid making a fist.

There's a restless shuffling from the line; people want to see what is happening but don't want to make themselves conspicuous. The inmate, still holding the deputy's gaze, says, "Nope. Don't wanna fuck with nobody."

The deputy backs off and says, "Good. That's good." Then he hollers, "Let's move. Next guy that talks misses tonight's gourmet dinner." The line moves briskly down the corridor, silent except for the padding of feet and the swishing of sleeves against the dull yellow wall.

¤ ¤ ¤

"Watchoo want, man, the cow turd loaf, or the pigshit sausage?" A huge biker with a beard to his chest and a net over his hair gestures toward two stainless steel pans full of equally unappealing choices. I point to the meatloaf. The biker scoops up a square with his spatula and dumps it on a plate.

"Enjoy."

"Yeah, thanks," I tell him, and go to the next counter. Here, I'm given what looks like mashed potatoes and a pile of shriveled peas. I pick an orange from a bowl, and a plastic cup, spoon, and fork from the next cart, and follow the man in front of me to a table.

There are about forty identical tables in the room, each with two rows of seven inmates facing each other. An enormous mural covers one wall—an underwater scene with whales and jellyfish, oddly serene as a backdrop to the roomful of dining criminals. When my table fills up, a trustee appears with two plastic pitchers of pale liquid that he sets down at the end of the table. A sudden clamor goes up: "Juice down." "Juice down!" "Hey, mothafuckah, juice down."

I prod the colorless square of alleged meat on my plate. For some reason the idea of eating appeals to me.

The pitcher arrives, nearly empty. I put it up to my face and sniff—Hawaiian Punch.

"Yo, mothafuckah, get yo' fuckin' Jew beak outta there. Juice down, man." It's the big guy who had the showdown with the guard. Probably still pissed off. I fill my glass and pass the pitcher to my right. Towering over the end of the table is the biker who served my meatloaf. The huge bearded man looks down at me, shaking his head in reproof. When the empty pitchers reach the end of the table, the man places them in a plastic tub on a rolling cart and goes on to the next group, still shaking his head.

¤ ¤ ¤

After dinner, I doze on my bunk, thinking about Mindy and trying to ignore the rumbling in my belly. I can feel the food moving through me in a lump. When it finally gets to be too much, I drop to the floor and walk down the corridor between the rows of bunks, past the open area where the brothers sit on hard benches, and toward the latrine section.

This is my second day as a deceased person, and I haven't sat on a toilet yet. There are eight stainless steel toilets lining a six-foot-high wall, perpendicular to which are eight urinals. Men sit on each of the toilets, bare to the ankles with their jumpsuits carefully undone and rolled down in such a way as to not touch the floor, which is wet throughout the section. The men look out expressionlessly over the common area.

There are two empty seats in a row. I choose the one at the end, unbutton my coveralls, and sit down, feeling slightly less conspicuous in the corner. I close my eyes and try to picture the process of food moving through my system. Something tells me that the meatloaf and peas might come out still meatloaf and peas.

I hear rustling and grunting noises coming from my left. Someone sits heavily and breaks wind like an M-80 in a trashcan. I open my eyes and look over: It's the biker from the mess hall. The man is a naked mountain of billowing white flesh, his huge belly pouring out over his lap as he hunches forward.

He turns his head and looks at me. With the net off, his hair spills wildly over his face and down his back. "Hey, fish, how'd you like your cow-turd patty?" He chuckles and farts again.

I shrug. I really don't feel like conversing at the moment.

"Hey, man, I saw you and that jig with the big muscles in the mess hall. You know you can't let the niggers fuck with you that way." I notice a tattoo on the guy's arm. A blond-maned Conan the Barbarian type skewers a caricature of a black man with the sharp end of a flagpole. Above the stars and stripes are the words "Aryan Nation" in an ornate script. "You hang with us and jigs'll leave you alone, that's fer damn fuckin' sure."

I say, "I'm not hangin' with anybody, man. I'm outta here." Which I have no idea is true. I guess I'll get arraigned tomorrow, but I can't afford a lawyer.

"Yeah, well, next time then. You come check us out next time."

"There won't be any next time," I say.

The bearded guy says, "Yeah, right, and I'm here 'cause they got the wrong fuckin' guy. Hey, you're not really a fuckin' Jew, are you?"

I look at the biker, his hairy face and the mad-dog gleam in his eye, and say, "What's the matter, you don't like them either?"

The biker looks away, grunts, and voids his bowels in a wet explosion. "Fuckin' jail food."

Chapter 12

It's three in the morning and I'm standing on Bauchet Avenue outside of the county jail. I start walking. There are no buses and I have no cash for a ride. No magic cabbie is going to appear out of the blue, unless Daniel got processed out even quicker than I did. At least I got my stuff my back. I fish my cell phone from my pocket; the battery is dead. With any luck, I'll get mugged and finally hit the bullshit trifecta.

Lights from behind me. A silver BMW pulls up to the curb, the window hums down, and Tanya leans across the passenger seat and says, "Come on," as she opens the door. When I get in she stomps on the gas and we blast off into the bleak, sodium-lit LA night.

"So, Charlie, you're kind of an accident waiting to happen, aren't you?" She runs a red light without blinking and puts her hand on my knee. "What are we ever going to do with you?" Her hand moves up my leg and long red fingernails do a little scratch dance on my thigh.

I tell her I need to use her phone. We hit the onramp to the Santa Monica Freeway doing close to ninety. She reaches in her purse, but instead of a cellphone she pulls out an amber vial with a little spoon attached to the cap. She unscrews the cap and helps herself to a healthy snort in each nostril. I don't need a wakeup but go through the motions anyway.

Her cellphone is so tricked out you need a technical degree to turn it on, but I manage to dial Mindy's number. I get her voicemail and tell her I'm on my way home, try me at the number on her caller ID.

"Charlie, you've been through a lot. I've got a room at the Oceana. Whoever you're calling is probably sleeping anyway." Her hand moves up even further and gives me a little pat. She says, "You deserve a break. Call it a celebration of your new freedom."

There's not much else to do at three in the morning. This could be interesting.

¤ ¤ ¤

The Oceana is more like a luxury condo than a hotel, although you can rent by the night. I could live like this, nice furniture, ocean view, don't have to own anything and it still feels like home. I have to wonder about Tanya's bankrupt husband and the credit card bill, but hey, I just work here.

Tanya seems to have quite an affair going with the nose candy. She hit on it three more times on the way here. Now she brings two glasses and a bottle of Chivas. I watch her pour three fingers for each of us and drain hers like it's Gatorade after a hard run. She's in party mode and hasn't mentioned the reports once. Another snort from the vial and she excuses herself and leaves the room.

I give the room a once-over. The walls are covered with woven bamboo; the décor is a weird blend of modern and traditional. Gleaming wood floors, abstract art, and over-stuffed furniture. A glass-top table with magazines, sitting on a Turkish rug. I pull up a corner of the rug and slide the reports under it. I let the corner back down and check to make sure nothing shows.

I sit on the sofa thinking it would be fun to roam into the other room and watch Tanya, but the sound of bare feet padding on the wood floor tells me she's coming back. Music pops on, the African reggae guy who got killed when some punks carjacked him in Johannesburg. "Lucky" somebody. Or not. And now here's Tanya standing over me in a silk thigh-length robe. She has a lighted joint that smells like the high-grade hydro that Jimmy sells. She bends down and puts her open mouth on mine and softly pushes smoke into me.

She straddles me, takes one more hit off the joint and puts it in an ashtray, then puts her lips to mine again. Her eyelashes are nearly gone, but the line between exotic and weird has always been a thin one for me. Her left hand is moving between her legs. She moans as she lets go another cloud of smoke into my mouth. I put my hand on her ass, which is gyrating in time to the music. She reaches out with her right hand and touches my ear with the tips of her nails. Her hand moves up and I deflect it before she gets to my wound. I wouldn't want to destroy the mood for her.

She takes my hand and places it between her legs. It's warm and slick and I find the spot and gently rotate the ball of my middle finger on it. She's breathing into my ear, her face falls to my shoulder, she turns and bites my neck. I'm watching the silk robe ride up toward the middle of her back, the perfection of her little body, and wondering if I can make things work.

Tanya pulls back and looks down into my eyes. The robe falls open and her breasts point up and away from me.

She says, "Holy shit am I high."

"Me too. Great stuff." A perfect lie. Can't feel a thing.

"Charlie Miner, there's something spooky about you; I don't know what it is, but it makes me hot." She scoots backward off the sofa and leans down to undo my trousers. She pulls off my shoes and socks, then my pants and boxers, and puts out her hand. I take it and she leads me to the bedroom. I look down at myself and concentrate and bingo! It looks like I'm equipped for the job.

She falls backward onto the bed and pulls me down on top of her. She writhes and whimpers and twitches and moans and looks like a dream. We carry on for hours; the candles burn out and first light appears in the curtained windows. She brings me another drink and I down it. In my condition, I have the sex drive of a neutered lab monkey, but I persist for the sheer narcissistic pleasure of watching her.

¤ ¤ ¤

I topple off of her as if exhausted and lay on my side next to her, taking deep breaths. I let my breathing subside and fake a twitch. I feel her hand on my shoulder. It brushes up my neck and rests right on top of the bullet hole. She whispers, "Lights out, baby."

I lay still as she gets up. I hear the sounds of clothes being picked up and put on, a zipper closing, a brush through her hair. I feel her watching me.

She leaves the room. I leave the body and follow. As I expect, she goes straight for my clothes on the floor and picks up my pants. She pulls out my wallet and looks through it, then throws it aside. She turns my pockets inside out, then checks the pockets of my jacket and throws it on the ground and says, "Fuck! Fuck! Fuck!" She stomps around in a little circle and bangs her fist on the sofa.

I follow as she walks to the kitchen counter. Her cell phone is there, next to her car keys and purse. She picks up the phone and thumbs a number and taps an angry rhythm on the counter while she waits.

"He doesn't have it." Her tapping gets spastic in its intensity while she listens to the other end.

"How the fuck should I know? I thought this would be a snap. Look, I'm beat. I haven't slept in two days. I'm going to take a couple of Ambien and check out."

The tapping stops and now silence.

"Nah, I put two roofies in his drink. He'll be out for way longer than me. Don't worry about it." She taps the phone off and rummages through her purse. I watch as she takes out two 10mg Ambiens and swallows them dry. She pours herself another drink from the bottle of Chivas, kicks off her shoes, and settles back onto the sofa.

¤ ¤ ¤

There's nothing to do until she falls asleep. I move around, watching her from different angles as she drinks, scratches her chin, checks her text messages, and finally lets her head fall back against the cushions. She stares at the ceiling, slowly shakes her head and says, "Jesus Fucking Christ," and then closes her eyes.

There's something wrong and I don't know what it is. I feel disoriented. Edgy, and almost dizzy. For a moment I don't know how to get back to my body. When I get there it doesn't seem to want to let me in. Maybe I was out too long. Maybe the roofies really did affect me. Or the weed and the booze. I don't know, but I nearly panic for a second. It's not something I ever want to feel again.

There's an iPad on the table, and on an impulse I take Daniel's card out of my pocket. It has his name on it, along with a logo. The logo is the mandala from the man's hat in my dream. Below it is the inscription "Recover or Die." Below that, embossed in silver, it says "Second Chance at Life" and gives a website address. I pull up the site on the iPad.

Second Chance at Life is a treatment program for heroin addicts. It uses a hallucinogen called ibogain, in combination with other psychotropic drugs, along with ritual

70

chanting and drumming, to induce a state that is supposed to release the addict from the desire to use. It's illegal—because of the ibogain—in the US, so they have facilities all over the place: Brazil, Switzerland, the Caribbean, and Mexico.

Mexico.

Out of curiosity, I tap the image of the mandala. It fills the screen and begins to move, generating new patterns from its center that move outward in concentric circles.

Like a kaleidoscope.

And I remember.

¤ ¤ ¤

They gave me a last fix: a dose of morphine from an ampule just before we crossed the border. It was so strong that I nodded out for most of the drive to the clinic. I had picked the program because it promised to be painless and was supposed to be over in a couple of days. They told me their recovery rate was over eighty percent.

We crossed from El Paso. Even as high as I was, I could feel the tension in the car as we drove through Juarez. In the late afternoon, after driving for miles through Chihuahua desert, we arrived at a farmhouse.

Daniel was my driver. Daniel was the man who brought the cup in my dream.

Chapter 13

Dead plus two roofies should put me a few notches past comatose, but driving Tanya's BMW M6 Coupe makes me feel like I'm seventeen and joyriding in my old man's Vette. I got in a pile of trouble for that, but he's the one that totaled the car in an alcoholic blackout. Best of luck, Pop, wherever you are.

I left Tanya snoring on the sofa, her mouth open and one eyelid fluttering. Not her best look, but convenient for me. I took her keys and cell phone and recovered the reports from under the rug. If I had been smart, I would have grabbed some cash since I've got none, but I'm coming up to the Venice Boulevard off-ramp and there's no turning back. There's no return call from Mindy, but she never gets up this early.

It's 6:45 in the morning and the beginning of another muggy August day. Traffic is still light. I head east on Venice and turn up my street, same as I did when I rode my bike with the attaché case. I can picture the Mustang creeping up behind me. The guy in the passenger seat looks familiar. My mind stops there.

My house.

Gone.

I pull into the driveway and look at the charred foundation, like a rotten stump of a tooth in an otherwise healthy smile of nice little white houses. There's a pile of bricks surrounding the base of what was once my chimney.

I grab Tanya's phone and text Mindy: **Where are you? Call me ASAP**

The front door of the house next to mine opens and my neighbor comes out. He's a black ex-Marine, built like a heavyweight boxer, and has a kid that looks just like him. He crosses his lawn and comes up to me.

"Nice car."

"Yeah, new girlfriend. Have you seen Mindy?"

"Not since before the fire."

"The fire. What fire?" We're both staring at the slag heap that was once my home. Crows perch on the chimney stump, claiming the property as their own.

Calvin shakes his head and whistles. "You've always got some goofy shit goin' on, but this is a real jackpot." Funny, I always thought I was the nice, quiet neighbor.

Cal hasn't liked me ever since he found his wife prancing around my living room buck naked on a hot Friday afternoon. She had appeared at my door dressed in a raincoat with nothing on underneath and barged in demanding, "Fuck me, Charlie, I know you've always wanted to. My husband stinks of beer and cigars." She told Cal that I had stuck my head over the backyard fence and interrupted her nude sunbathing to invite her to my house for a drink.

"Thanks, Cal, I appreciate the sympathy. Now, what the hell happened here?"

"Night before last, around midnight, my dog starts barking. Wakes me up." Calvin's got a noisy Rottweiler that I would gladly shoot if they made a big enough gun.

"Yeah, did you put on your cammies and crawl outside with a knife in your teeth?"

Calvin grins down at me like I'm a chump about to get pounded behind the bleachers. "Cop said you were in the county jail."

"Cop, what cop? Why the fuck would he tell you that?"

"Man was in the Corps. Share intel. Semper Fi 'n all that shit."

"Jesus, Cal, just tell me what happened."

"So I look out my window and see a car pulled up in front of your house. Driver stays in the car. Small guy gets out. Funny lookin', even in the dark. He goes to your front door, then goes around to the side of the house. Had a bag full of some kinda shit with him."

"Yeah, what kind of car?"

"Silver Mustang. Ten minutes later he comes out with Mindy and they drive off."

"What do you mean, 'comes out with Mindy'? Was he forcing her?"

"She was walking in front of him. I told the cops it looked like he might have had a gun."

"Why, did you see one?" The guy's irritating me and enjoying himself. I want to slam open my car door on him and jump out and annihilate him on the charred remains of my lawn, but I stay cool. After all, he's sharing intel. And I need to save my rage for its proper target.

"No," he says. "But ten minutes later your house looked like the fuckin' Reichstag." He reaches in his pocket, pulls out a business card, and hands it to me through the window. "Cop says you know him and to give you this." He lights a cigar and walks away.

I look at the card: it says "Sergeant Dave Putnam, LAPD." My pal Dave, the writing detective. The guy's got more stories than a pack of Nigerian scam artists, and he turns them all into novels. He writes on a laptop during coffee breaks, stakeouts, and during all his time off. I wouldn't be surprised if he types while he craps. I know all this because we used to go to the same kickboxing gym and would do Starbucks or Rubio's afterward. I even helped him close a homicide case once.

So Ratboy's got Mindy. Too bad he couldn't have taken my ex instead.

Chapter 14

I know I should be furious, frantic, ballistic even, but
instead I just feel focused. I'm a laser-guided missile
looking for my target. Locate, lock, and launch. Except
that I have no idea where to start looking.

Time to get moving.

I call Mindy's cell on Tanya's phone and get voicemail
again. There's a charger in my car for my own cell, so I
head back to Jimmy's building and hope that the Z is still
in the underground parking.

I've got no cash, no home, I'm fresh out of jail, my pal's
in the hospital, and my daughter has been kidnapped by a
probable killer for reasons having to do with an investment
scam and a bogus geology report, all stemming from a visit
just a few days ago from a beautiful Eurasian stranger with
a story. Oh yeah, and I'm clinically dead, with a bullet hole
in my head to prove it. Jimmy's Hummer is gone, probably
towed and searched for drugs. My old Z is still sitting in its
spot, rusty and battered but the only home I've got. I plug
in my cell but have to wait for it to charge some before I
can use it.

Tanya's BMW got me to Jimmy's on fumes and the Z
gauge is in the red. I'm a moron for not borrowing some
cash from Tanya's purse, but here I am, two fine steeds
and no oats.

I fire up the Z and head back out to Washington Boulevard. I've got no plan, but the car seems to know where it's going. A few blocks and I'm at Mo's 7-Eleven.

¤ ¤ ¤

I'm standing in the alley next to the trash trying to think. The soggy August winds are wafting through the garbage and the air is hot and ripe.

"Charlie! Hey Charlie, for God's sake!" Mo yells at me from the back door. He's not happy about our arrangement, but has agreed to give me thirty bucks in gas and ten in cash if I work for him till noon. I already put the gas in the Z. His regular guy didn't show, so Mo needed me. Meanwhile, I'm going nuts. No calls from Mindy, can't reach her mom, zip, zero, nada.

"Hey, Goddammit, I need two cases of Michelob out front right now. What the hell are you doing?"

"I just took out the trash," I tell him. If I had been smoking a cigarette he wouldn't have asked.

"Come on, man, I need that beer." He's standing in the doorway; I can't go through until he moves.

"What's the secret word?" He asks me, fingering an invisible cigar.

"Fuck, Mo, I don't know. Mackerel? Allah? There's a hole in my head so I forgot."

"You know what, Charlie? You are a very strange guy."

I think about a time when I was small, my first day at a new school. I was walking across the blacktop when I noticed a speck in the sky. A bird, I thought. It grew larger. I stopped. It seemed to be flying to me. As I watched, it gained speed and then hit me on the forehead. An older boy had thrown a rock from the other side of the playground. So I want to say *It's Life itself that's strange, Mo, not me.* But instead I just tell him, "You don't know the half of it."

"I calls 'em like I sees 'em," he says.

"Win a few, lose a few, right?"

"Hey, like I always say, nobody's perfect, ya follow what I'm sayin'?"

When I was a teenager, I worked at an impound yard in Oakland, with the Dobermans and the wrecked cars. Every morning was the same: "Hey, big guy, how they hangin'?" And I knew to say, "Hangin' loose, Walt." Walt, who owned the yard, would say, "Well don't let your meat loaf." I'd say, "No way, Jose." Then the other guys would laugh and Walt would ask, "Hey Charlie, what time is it on the equator?" And when I'd answer, "Could be anytime, Walt, anytime at all," he would tell the guys, "Ya gotta get up mighty early to fool Charlie," like I was some dimwit they could all mess with.

"When you're done with the beer I need you to get to the magazine racks. Fucking kids got 'em all messed up again," Mo says over his shoulder. I already did the racks. Great stuff there: "DOG-FACED MAN MAR-RIES WORLD'S HAIRIEST WOMAN!,""ABDUCTED WOMAN GIVES BIRTH TO TWIN ETs," and "FAITH HEALER CURES MOVIE STAR WITH CRYSTALS!"

The beer is in the storeroom, which is also the office. The room itself is a mess, but I know where everything is. For example, the Michelob is against the far wall, which is north from the doorway. Domestic beers line the west wall, except for where the desk is. I get the Michelob and take it out to Mo.

"Thanks, Charlie. Listen, catch the racks later. Some kid just dropped a bottle of SoBe over by the video games. Gotta get it mopped up. Get all the goddamn glass, OK?"

"You got it, Mo," I tell him, and head back for the storeroom, where the mop is.

In the storeroom, I'm about to reach for the mop, but I'm really thinking about the desk. It's cluttered on top with paperwork and receipts, candy bar wrappers and Styrofoam coffee cups. I sit down in front of it—on the wall in front of me is a calendar. A girl with enormous breasts spilling out of a bikini sits on a motorcycle, looking through me and smiling. She's part Asian, and a chill of rage goes through me as I see Tanya, taunting me from the chopper.

In the top right drawer is a gun. I take it out. It's a Walther P38-K and the clip is full. I put it back and close the drawer.

Another time, during college, I worked in one of those little photo huts in a supermarket parking lot. FAST-FOTO, it was called. I would look at the pictures and then seal them back in their packets. The people would come. A packet to the worried-looking woman in the beat-up sedan. Her pictures were of a young girl in a leg-brace walking on the beach, blowing out candles, opening presents, and smiling on a playground swing; in this last shot the brace is right out front. A packet to the teenage boy in a Jeep, with its loud, rumbling engine. He seemed to like taking photos of marijuana plants. They were in a series: growing in the yard, hanging upside-down from a clothesline, drying in the sun, and, finally, stuffed neatly into clear bags and displayed on a bed. A packet to the man in the red sports car—he had photographs of turds in a toilet, six of them. Photos, that is. The rest were of his car in a driveway. And Mo calls me strange.

I'm losing focus. I wheel the mop and bucket out to the game area. It's packed into a corner, past the magazines, at the end of the aisle where the canned goods are. Three kids are playing at the games, dressed alike in jeans and long tee shirts. They all have the same sneakers and haircuts, short on the sides, spiky on top. I try to move into position to clean up the SoBe under the middle machine, *Invisible Enemy.*

"Hey, Pop, you're messin' up my game."

"I have to clean up under there," I tell him.

"I got high score of the day and three fuckin' rockets left, dude," says the kid. These kids could play forever on one quarter. I mop at the edge of the puddle by his foot.

"You better not mess with Bobby's game," says one of the other boys, who just now ended his own battle with *RoboCop.* He looks about sixteen. I'm thinking it's time to call Mo, but instead I push the wet mop up against Bobby's tennis shoe.

"Hey! You mess with my game I'll fuck you up," Bobby says without looking up. He has a gold hoop in his ear. I yank the cord on the machine and bend Bobby over so his forehead touches the panel.

"Bobby?" I whisper, "Can you hear me?"

He tries to nod. His friends are edged up against the racks.

"Bobby, I am the Invisible Enemy and you're all out of ships. What do you want to do?"

"Nothing, man. Let me go."

"Bobby, I've been resurrected from the dead. What do you think of that?" I ask him.

"Nothin'. I think you're a fuckin' wacko." He's struggling now, but I have more to say.

"Wrong, Bobby. It's life that's wacko, son. It's not me. Chew on that for a while. Here . . ." I straighten him up. I hand him the mop and slap a quarter on the game counter. "Try to get all of the glass."

I turn around and walk down the aisle, past the magazines, past paper plates and Lipton tea, past the carousel with the sunglasses, past Mo, who's punching up fifty dollars worth of Lotto tickets for an old lady—she buys her food here with welfare stamps—and on into the office. I take off my apron. The drawer sticks shut and for a moment I worry that it's locked, but then it opens.

I'm in the parking lot now, the gun stuck in my pants. As I start my car I see Mo looking up from the register, a puzzled expression on his face.

Sorry, Mo.

Chapter 15

I put the gun in my glove box. It would be legal in my trunk, but the Z doesn't have one. My cellphone barks and I snatch at it. Caller ID tells me it's a private number. I put it on speakerphone and clip it to my visor so I won't get stopped for using it while driving.

"Sweatin' a little?" A high, nasal voice, male. I know the voice, but I can't place it.

"Who is this?"

"This is Jason Hamel. You've got something I want, I've got something you want, and I'm tired of fuckin' around." If this is Jason Hamel, he's thrown out his scripture-quoting, righteous Christian act like it's last night's Halloween costume.

"Where's my daughter? Put her on the phone, now."

"Listen, you freak, I don't know how you survived a bullet in your head, but I should have put another one between your eyes." A whiney snarl in my ear, hard to square with the silver-maned gent on the website.

Confronted with my killer, I can only blurt, "MINDY . . . NOW," a spastic shout while I swerve to avoid an SUV full of kids in baseball uniforms trying to make a left turn through the light that I was running. The Z's on its own now, skidding at an angle until it mashes into a parked pickup truck full of furniture. The guy driving the SUV rolls down a window and yells, "What, are you crazy?" and drives away. I watch as the pickup driver starts to get out of his truck.

The voice on the phone says, "Stew on it a bit longer, bitch," and clicks off. I do the prudent thing under the circumstances and peel out, heading toward the coast.

¤ ¤ ¤

It's a hot and crowded day at the beach. I have to park off Main on Brooks and walk because I don't have any money for beach-lot parking. I cut through a river of people milling on the boardwalk and past the park where the Rollerbladers skate to music blasting from a portable PA system and skateboarders perform tricks on a wooden ramp.

At the shoreline, children are wading in the shallow water. A skinny man in oversize flowered trunks stands knee deep in the surf; I watch a wave hit him in the chest and knock him over. I'm wandering now, still without a plan, clutching my cell phone and waiting for Jason Hamel to let me talk to my daughter.

I head south on the boardwalk, caught in the current of tourists and locals, hustlers and crazies, and other regulars roaming the strip between the shops and the beach. Kids dressed up like hippies from the sixties are hanging out, the girls wearing tie-dyes and granny glasses. Cops follow close on the heels of a group of five black teenagers wearing baggy pants, oversize tee shirts, and identical basketball shoes. A turbaned man playing a guitar glides by on Rollerblades, weaving through the slow-moving crowd.

To my right, on the perimeter of the sand, are the vendors, their wares laid out on colorful blankets; jewelry and carved wood, stone pipes with screens in them, pottery, and herbal health potions. I navigate around a knot of people crowded around two jugglers throwing flaming kerosene-dipped torches, a volunteer onlooker now standing in the line of fire as the burning sticks sail behind and in front of him, only inches away. Wild-eyed panhandlers pick on the tourists at the edge of the throng.

North of Thornton, the crowd thins out. I'm about to turn back when I notice a familiar figure in the sand. He looks up and grins.

"Hey, my mon, Charlie, I been waiting on you." It's Daniel, sitting at a card table full of small prisms and colored-glass pyramids. At the center of the table is a deck of odd-looking cards and a placard that says, "Past, present, future, right here, right now, only ten dollars."

"Sit down, sit down. Good to see you, mon." Daniel gestures for me to sit in the empty chair at his table. A bearded dwarf wearing only speedos and wraparound sunglasses is bearing down on me, pulling a cart with a legless man playing a Cajun waltz on an accordion. Daniel whistles and says, "Some mighty strange people we got here. And I seen plenty strange."

"I'll bet you have," I say, taking a seat. "I don't have time for chit-chat. I'm in a jam, big time."

Daniel grins again and says, "Charlie Miner, battling de forces of evil, all by himself." Why he thinks this is funny, I don't know, but it's pissing me off.

I gesture toward the prisms and cards on the table. "So what's up with this bullshit?"

"Props, mon, all for show."

"Props?" I turn over the top card of the deck. It shows a man hanging upside down. Or is the card upside down?

"De white mon don't believe in direct knowledge of de hidden world. So he need to see juju, voodoo, mumbo jumbo. Props..." He makes a gesture of dismissal at the items on the table. "They are not necessary for seeing."

"And what do you see for me? Somebody's got to see something, because I'm flying blind."

"For you?" Daniel locks eyes with mine, seeming to stare right into me. "In you I see a sickness of de mind and spirit." He pauses and seems to consult some inner voice. "Give me your hand."

I hesitate. I don't need some charlatan's crap about my planets being out of alignment. On the other hand, this guy has definitely got an angle I've never seen before. I let him take my hand.

A current passes between us, powerful but gentle. Daniel grips my hand and closes his eyes, then opens them and says, "Commune with your spirit to begin healing."

"Commune with my spirit?"

"You've been given a chance to heal. Death hasn't been allowed to touch you. Do not leave your body for too long, or He will have his way and collect you." Totally uninflected English, without a hint of an accent.

"What's too long?" And how does Daniel know about roaming?

"You will know. You can feel it when it's close." I remember the panic that almost took me at Tanya's hotel room. Daniel's hand relaxes and lets go of mine.

"That's it?"

"For now, yes."

"They have my daughter."

"Yes, the man who took your life."

"How do you know that?"

Daniel laughs, then shrugs. "I see it."

"I know who you are now."

"That's good. We've been worried about you."

"What happened to me?"

"You were part of the twenty percent."

"What's that supposed to mean?"

"We have an eighty percent recovery rate. Four out of five of our patients are clean after a year."

"And the twenty percent...?"

"Well..." Daniel picks up the hanging-man card and shows it to me. "Some have psychotic breaks and are never the same, and some completely repress the whole experience. Like you. We brought you home and I watched you go back to using as if nothing had ever happened."

"How does all this explain my condition?"

"There's no answer to that, except that we've seen it before."

"There are others?"

"Yes, Charlie Miner. You're looking at one."

There's nothing left to say.

I look up as Daniel nods toward the passing carnival. A pair of female body builders approaches, hard round breasts pushing against identical British-flag bikini tops. One of them is carrying a Chihuahua, taut and wiry, against her muscular tan body.

I shake my head after the women pass. "You know what they say about making love to a gorilla?"

"What's dat?" Now he's back to doing the Rasta thing.

"You're not through until the gorilla's through."

Daniel grins and says, "Dat's what dey say about heroin."

"Yeah, it's like that too."

Chapter 16

Tanya's phone chirps in my pocket. I don't recognize the number, but then why should I? I flip it open anyway and Tanya screams at me. I'm walking up Brooks, back to my car, listening to her rant about stealing her car and how dare I fuck her and run after she got me out of jail. I wait until she runs out of steam and say, "Sounds like you finally got a good night's sleep, sweetheart."

"Don't you sweetheart me, asshole. I'm calling the cops."

"I've got a better idea. Why don't you tell me exactly where this Jason Hamel lives so I can try and get my daughter back that he KIDNAPPED AFTER BURNING DOWN MY FUCKING HOUSE?" I'm screaming now, and people are stopped on the sidewalk and staring at me.

A big tourist in an "I Love Venice Beach" tee shirt says, "Hey fella, watch your language." He's shielding his wife and two little kids as if I'm a hyena loose from the zoo. I keep walking.

"He what?" Tanya sputters. I repeat myself, quietly this time. Save the rage. Focus.

"That's crazy, Charlie, he's not like that at all."

I tell her Cal's version of the fire and about the phone call.

"He called you a bitch? He must have gone completely insane. What are you going to do?"

"As soon as you tell me where he lives, I'm going to track his sorry ass down and make this right." Now there's a plan to admire, but I do have at least one useful tool on my side. Like I'm not afraid of guns.

"Charlie..."

"I don't want to hear it."

"I need my car. And my phone. And I'm sorry."

I tell her where the BMW is, keys under the seat. Can't help her with the phone, I'm on a mission. She gives me an address: 2412 East Rustic Road in Santa Monica Canyon.

She's sorry.

¤ ¤ ¤

What's really sorry is the condition of the Z, with its front end all mashed in and the hood buckled. And the parking ticket. But who gives a shit at this point?

I buckle up and take off, turning north on Main. Rustic Canyon is a neighborhood embedded in Santa Monica Canyon, a funky-rich world of its own between the beach and Sunset Boulevard.

My phone barks. My ex-wife. I'm not in the mood, but she might have heard from Mindy. I flip the phone open.

"You fucking prick! I call your home line, your office line, your fucking cell phone, Mindy's cell, and nobody has the courtesy to fucking pick up?" She's snarling at me. I should be used to it but I'm not. It's why I left. It's why Mindy had to leave. Sober, Allison is cold and sharp and keeps her acid voice level. I prefer her drunk.

"I thought she was with you." Truth, the first casualty of war, and the white flag is in shreds. I hang up.

Tanya's phone rings. I'm heading down the California Incline toward the Pacific Coast Highway. Caller ID says "Alan Hunter." Might be an interesting conversation, but now's not the time.

A right on Entrada gets me into the Canyon. A few twists and turns and I'm on East Rustic, which dead-ends at 2412. A jungle of sycamore and ivy, out of control Korean boxwood hedge competing with bougainvillea, an open gate and a long curving driveway.

I take the Z slow up the bumpy driveway, crunching gravel. I get past a bend to the right and see the house, a traditional Spanish bungalow restored to showcase condition in the midst of vegetation gone wild. Under a picture window, up against the house, there's a perfectly tended rose garden. I turn off the engine and hear dogs yapping. I pull the gun from my glove compartment, tuck it in my pants, and button my jacket to cover it.

Dogs yap furiously as I approach the door. It opens before I knock. I'm standing face to face with a mild-mannered gent, slender with silver hair and round, wire-rimmed glasses. He's wearing an Argyle cardigan sweater, gray flannels, and oxblood loafers with shiny pennies in them. Old school. The dogs are golden cocker spaniels and they shut up when the guy makes a little gesture with his hand.

"Can I help you?" This is not the guy who told me to "stew on it a bit longer, bitch." Who said he was Jason Hamel. But he is the guy from the mining website, which makes him the real Jason Hamel. Identity theft? Multiple Personality Disorder? I'm clearing my throat and trying to decide whether to pull out my gun or apologize for bothering him, but he glances over at my car and says, "You must be Mr. Miner. Come in, please."

I follow him into an attractive, bright, and spacious living room. The picture window looks out on a short yard and a view of the canyon. Hamel gestures for me to sit on the sofa. My back is to the window. He sits opposite me in a richly upholstered dark leather chair.

"I hope you brought the documents?" He says, businesslike, but pleasant. The gun wants to come out, but I keep my cool.

"The documents aren't the issue right now, Mr. Hamel. My daughter has been kidnapped and nothing else is going to happen until she's safe with me."

He stares at me, blinking furiously, then looks down at his feet. He pulls a cell phone out of his pocket, hits some keys, and hands it to me.

"Is this your daughter?"

And there's Mindy, her black eye makeup smeared, her hair wild with its streak of green, looking at the camera like a feral cat about to reach out and slash someone.

"Where did you take this?"

"I didn't take it. It was sent to my phone."

"So who sent it?" I'm not fond of games on the best of days.

"My son, Jason. He texted me that this is the girl he intends to marry." His expression transforms from a prim belligerence to sadness, as if he has just resigned himself to some awful truth. He takes back the phone and hits a button and hands it back to me.

Now I'm looking at Mindy and a character, standing with his arm around her, that my mind rejects entirely. In fact, my mind rejects Hamel, his dogs, and his living room.

¤ ¤ ¤

I was four houses away from my own, cruising on booze and heroin in the warm night, the empty attaché case in my left hand, the bike on autopilot, when the silver Mustang pulled up next to me. I noticed the driver first because he looked like a gorilla, hunched over so that his head would clear the ceiling, his eyes as dark and dumb as buttons on a coat. In the same split second I saw Ratboy, low in the passenger-side window, and suddenly, impossibly, a gun, a pop, a sting at my temple, and I flew off the bike onto the grass between the sidewalk and the curb.

I lay there and heard a car door open. Footsteps, then the attaché case, which for some reason I still gripped, yanked from my hand. A nasal voice said, "Fuck you, turkey." A car door slammed. The roaring in my head began.

¤ ¤ ¤

I can still feel the grass on my cheek. Through the noise, I hear my name being called. I see light, and the anxious face of Jason Hamel.

"Are you all right?" He's leaning forward, half out of his chair with his hand extended.

"Yeah, low blood sugar, no problem." I wave him back into his chair and consider my revelation. Ratboy put the bullet in my head, and Ratboy's got Mindy.

"You sat there, immobile, staring through me for over two minutes. Can I get you anything?"

"Forget about me. Where's your son now?"

"Why, he's on his way here. He called me about twenty minutes ago."

"If that's your boy, your wife must be a strange looking creature."

"My wife died two years ago. Jason was adopted when he was two. His mother was an amphetamine addict. We tried to raise him in the way of the Lord, but another power has kept its grip on him."

The echo of the hurricane in my head reminds me that I'm in uncharted territory. A silver Mustang. The car that took Mindy away.

"Your son shot at me and kidnapped my daughter. I believe he burned my house down. What do you propose I do when he gets here?"

"You'll do what you have to do, I imagine. He's beyond reasoning with."

"What do I need to know?"

"He has a sidekick that drives him everywhere, since he can't drive himself. Big brute, dumb as dirt, has a violent streak, and is entirely loyal to Jason."

"Why can't Jason drive?"

"He got arrested for the seventh time. Oxycodone and cocaine." He looks at me apologetically. "A couple of sexual assault charges. I bailed him out every time. The best lawyers. This time he got two years probation plus a suspended license. He's fresh out of rehab, a condition of his probation."

The dogs prick up their ears in unison. I hear the crunch of tires on gravel and car doors slam shut. The dogs begin to yap and scramble around the table. Hamel stands up and turns to face the foyer. I stand and watch the front door open and Ratboy enter. I pull Mo's gun from under my belt and point it at Hamel's prodigal son. The dogs shut up and there's a moment of silence.

"Well, if it isn't dead man walking. We should kiss and make up, since you're my future father-in-law." He sneers and winks at the same time, an especially bad combination on his ugly face. I notice he has a lazy eye that seems to be looking at the tip of his nose.

I raise Mo's Walther and pull back the hammer. I don't know how heavy the pull on the trigger is, but I'm just a twitch away from blowing Ratboy's head off.

"Where's Mindy? That's all that's going to happen now—you're going to tell me where she is and we're going to go find her. Got it?"

Ratboy smirks and his good eye moves past me and over my shoulder. I hear shots as the window behind me explodes. I fire the Walther and Ratboy staggers backward, his hand clutched to his left shoulder. Two more shots from outside thwack into the living-room wall, and I hit the floor while Ratboy turns and runs out the door.

Tires on gravel.

Chapter 17

J ason Hamel Senior is lying on the floor facedown with a hole in his back, right about at kidney-level. There's blood pooling under him and he's scrabbling at the rug trying to push himself up.

"Help me, for God's sake."

I kneel down and pull his arm to his side and roll him over. His lips are drawn tight over clenched teeth but he says, "I want to sit up. Get me sitting up," so I maneuver him into a sitting position against the wall. I pull out my cell and start dialing for help.

"What are you doing?"

"Calling 911."

"There's no point. I'm not going to survive this. And I'm ready to meet my Lord." He gestures with one hand for me to put away my cell. "Funny, about your name. It's quite an irony."

"What about my name?"

"Miner. Charlie Miner. I've been in the business half my life. Always worked with miners. And here you are, a Miner to watch me die."

I shrug and say, "Irony, destiny, who knows?"

He reaches for the floor next to him and almost topples over. I help him back up and retrieve his glasses from the rug. He wipes them carefully on his ruined cardigan and puts them on. "Do you believe in destiny, Mr. Miner?"

"It seems all my beliefs are subject to review at the moment. Are you sure you don't want help?" Ambulance, police, interrogation: all would put time between me and finding Mindy. I'll call when I'm in the car.

He gives another little wave of dismissal and says, "I'm in His hands now. I believe in the Lord Jesus Christ, sent by our Father to absolve us of our sins."

"Will he absolve you of the murders of the Caffey brothers?"

"You think I did that? Why on Earth would you say that?" He's clutching his abdomen now, there's blood leaking between his fingers.

"It seems that accidental falling and suicide weren't very credible versions of their deaths. And, their dying was pretty convenient for your scheme. So come on, repentance is good for the soul, isn't that what they say?"

Hamel grimaces in pain. His dogs are on either side of him, their paws on his legs, whimpering. One takes a tentative lick at his hand. Hamel looks down for a moment, then looks back at me. He moves a hand to adjust his glasses, leaving a smear of blood on the lens. Finally he says, "They mocked the Lord, but they didn't deserve to die." He shakes his head, his face a mask of pain and regret.

"So how did they die?"

"I never imagined . . . Jason overheard me talking on the phone. I was angry with the Caffeys. They had signed off on a report that I didn't agree with."

"You mean about the gold?"

"Yes, the gold. There's a huge deposit there. I'm convinced of it. I saw it in a vision. It was going to fund my ministry, and they were going to ruin it."

"So you had them killed and created a fake document."

"No, no, no." He's getting pale now. His pants are soaked in blood and his voice is weakening. "Jason told me later that evening that I should stop worrying, that the

Lord would find a way to make everything right and that he would be the arm of the Lord. He was fresh out of rehab and carrying on about how he was right with Jesus. Then James died and it seemed like a crazy accident. And Mark, committing suicide. I should have seen it back then, but I was in complete denial."

"But you went ahead and dummied up a false report."

"I don't know what you're talking about." A tear drops to his cheek on the bloody-lens side. "I just wanted the report before the investors saw it. The Caffey brothers were mistaken. I was trying to salvage a dream."

We sit for a moment. The one dog's tongue takes another furtive lick, this time landing in the liquid redness seeping through.

It's almost time to go. I've got two more questions.

"Tell me about Tanya's money. Where is it now?"

"Tanya doesn't have any money. Her husband is a hopeless gambler and a drunk, but he was smart enough to have a pre-nup with her. The investment in Santa Clarita was his last chance at digging himself out of a deep hole. She was blackmailing me for the cash, and then I was supposed to show him the report so he would think his money was gone."

"What happened to it?"

"It's all in the ground, out . . ." He looks down at his hands, his mouth opening and closing like a fish. I feel bad, he's done me no direct harm, but now he's just a source and I need to squeeze him before he dies on me.

"So where would your psychopath son take my daughter?"

"He likes to camp at the project. He wanted to marry her there. He thinks it's a sacred place. He gets these ideas—sudden obsessions."

"The project?"

"The mine. Santa Clarita. I took him there once to help him detox. I baptized him in the stream. He said he found Jesus. Later I found out he was high on the local peyote." He's breathing through his mouth now, staring at me, his eyes wide. He says, "Thank you for staying with me." His stare loses focus. Both dogs give a startled jump and begin to whimper.

Chapter 18

The average police response time in this city is about nine minutes. Add a few for neighbors to scratch their heads and wonder if they should make the call. I'm probably out of time.

I reach for Hamel's wallet and a cocker snaps at my wrist. There are a few hundreds and some smaller bills, so I leave fifteen bucks and put the wallet back. There's a Blackberry in his pocket. Dog teeth break skin this time, but I'm betting it's worth it. As my former neighbor would say, intel.

I'm just turning onto West Channel Road when the black-and-whites fly past me, lights flashing and sirens blaring. The shotgun cop in the third car whips his head around and checks me out, but I'm moving west, turning south on the Coast Highway, and there's nobody behind me.

So, Ratboy's got Mindy and wants to marry her. I should be enraged, clenching my teeth and ready to swing an axe, but it seems that my condition has put a damper on how I feel about things. That's a good thing, because my temper has led to a lot of bad decisions in the past. Focus on the mission, that's my mantra now.

There's a vibration in my pocket, followed by a Hammond organ playing "Rock of Ages." I fish out Hamel's Blackberry and check the Caller ID. It says, "J Jr," which I presume to be Ratboy. On a hunch, I pull into the Santa Monica Pier parking lot and turn off the engine.

Bad luck would be that Ratboy's calling from a cell phone. Good luck and he's calling from a listed land line. I pull up an online reverse lookup directory and enter the number. And there's young Jason, right down the street in Venice.

Oakwood's a part of Venice I generally avoid. First they gentrified Ocean Park and pushed the poor people farther into Venice. Then they yuppified Venice and left Oakwood to the black and Hispanic communities, along with the gangs. Now rising property values are pushing these folks out toward Inglewood, but I'll bet there are still some Shoreline Crips and Venice 13s left.

I pull up in front of a crappy little apartment building named The Flora. There's a hydrant, but what's a parking ticket in my situation? I tuck Mo's gun in my belt and cover it with my jacket. The crappy little apartment building has its own crappy little lawn, with a fence separating it from the sidewalk. The gate is halfway off its hinge. Dogs bark in stereo as I walk through and scan the mailboxes. Sounds like a beast on the right side, a big angry howl punctuated by snarling and a rattling of the apartment door.

Every box has a name except number 11, so I'm guessing that's my man. I start up the stairway to the second floor but have to back down because a huge black woman is descending. She would be unpassable even if she turned sideways. Especially if she turned sideways. She's wearing purple tights and some kind of sequined poncho. She squints down at me and says, "He gone."

I say, "Who gone?"

She says, "Funny lookin' white boy, look like a rat, and his go-rillafren' and the trashy little white girl. They left 'bout ten minutes ago."

I back down to the landing and let her pass. I get back in the Z. It's getting dark out and I have no idea where to go. Mo's gun is pushing into my thigh so I dislodge it from my belt but keep it under my jacket. I close my eyes.

Now I'm looking back at myself sitting in the Z. I guess I went into roam mode on autopilot. I float up the stairs and through the door to number 11.

The place looks like an animal's cave. There's laundry all over the floor and the kitchen area is a mess. The sink is full of dishes and greasy water. There's a futon mat on the living room floor, but no pillow or blankets. I navigate to the bedroom and find a completely different world: every-thing in its place, miniature cars lined up in precision on a bookshelf; magazines on a table perfectly aligned with the corners; photographs of Jason Hamel Sr. and his son framed and hanging in perfect symmetry above a dresser topped with meticulously placed knickknacks and, as their centerpiece, a framed shot of the two Jasons and a woman, all smiling, Jason Junior's braces catching the light, his face pathetically happy and eager to please. Another shot shows Ratboy and his giant friend standing in front of a Chevy van, flashing gang signs. The big guy looks like he's been hit in the face with a brick, or perhaps his features never fully formed. And another of the woman, Ratboy's dead mother, with her thin, delicate face; her cheekbones, full lips, and unruly hair an unmistakable resemblance, at least in type, to my Mindy.

There's a desk in the corner, with a computer mon-itor. Google Earth is showing me a map of the Santa Clara Mountains, somewhere south of and inland from Ensenada. There's an image of a pushpin stuck next to a town called San Vicente and another one farther east. I feel a sudden weird panic and decide it's time to get back to my body, quickly.

¤ ¤ ¤

From the sidewalk I see a big guy wearing a bandana with his hand inside an oversize jacket, which is wrong already because it's a warm summer night. Another guy is leaning in my driver's side window.

I re-enter the body. The kid already has Jason's Black-berry, and now he's reaching around me to get at my wallet. All the while he's chattering away about dumb-ass white junkies and how they're messin' up the hood. I grab his shirt with my left hand and pull.

"Whoa, fuckin' let go a' me, Pops, or I'll fuck you up!" This is the second time I've heard this today, and I'm not very impressed.

"I think you're wearing your do-rag too tight, son." He tries to jerk away but I've got a solid grip on him. I see his friend move closer to the windshield and start to pull his hand out of his jacket.

"DeShaun," the kid yells. "Shoot the motherfucker!"

I've been holding on to Mo's gun the whole time; now I jam the barrel hard into the kid's head. "Tell DeShaun to give me his gun."

DeShaun is looking confused; he checks up and down the block, whether for cops or backup I don't know. The kid barks at him to give up the piece. When he gets to the window I tell him to reach in past his pal and drop it. DeShaun is about six four and has a big round face like a baby's. I tell him to cross the street, which he does, walking backward. When he's gone, I tell the kid to drop Jason's phone and get out of my car.

I've got Mo's gun in my left hand now, pointing out the window, and I start the Z and put it in gear. The kid's already talking trash, but I'm heading for the border.

Chapter 19

I've got two guns, three phones, and three hundred bucks and change. It's at least a couple hundred miles to where I'm going. Ratboy's got a half-hour lead on me, but I don't need to sleep or eat, so I might even catch up with him. Then what? A shootout at night on a Mexican highway with Mindy in the other car? And if I don't catch up? I've got the name of a town—San Vicente—and a pushpin icon in a map of a mountain range.

Jason's Blackberry rings. It's Ratboy. I let it go to voicemail and I text him: **cant talk**

A minute later I get back: **why not?**

I'm heading east on the Marina Freeway, toward the 5 South. I text back: **in bedroom—have a gun and im going to shoot the man**

The Blackberry chirps twice and I read: **fire the whole clip into his heart**

Another two chirps and: **then come to the mine and marry us**

I recall that Jason's web site mentioned that he was an ordained minister. I fire back: **ill call when its over**

I hate texting. I really hate people who text while driving. Now I am one. As an afterthought I type: **keep her pure**

And I get back: **till my wedding night**, with a smiley face.

I'll show you a smiley face.

¤ ¤ ¤

I've never liked Mexico, but then there are a lot of things I don't like. The 5 freeway ends at the border about two or three hours away, depending on traffic. Then there's Tijuana to get through.

Every Southern California junkie knows Tijuana. Like Daniel said, doing H is like having sex with a gorilla. You're not done till the gorilla's done. Junkies and pill-heads cross the border daily for the cheap fix. Walk across and turn right at the taxi stand and you'll find a row of tourist shops with the lamest inventories of dust-covered unsellable crap—plaster statues of Jesus, wood carvings of dolphins, unplayable ukuleles, goofy sombreros with four-foot brims—and a skinny dark guy with a gold tooth and matching cross behind the register. He's like the guy at a fancy uptown club: get past him and you can get to where the action is.

A nod by skinny-gold-tooth-guy will get you a pass to the shooting gallery in the next room, where you can order up any combination of goodies at cartel retail. Credit is a very bad idea, unless you want to leave some fingers behind.

I didn't start out a junkie. Most of them start out as kids partying on booze and weed. Then they get bored and experiment with more exotic stuff. Acid, Ecstasy, DMT, you name it. Then coke and speed, which means downers for the end of the ride: Xanax and Oxy. When the balancing act gets too tricky, the first snort of heroin solves the whole riddle of how to get right. It's no longer a question of how to get high, it's a matter of simply trying to feel human again. Heroin can do that. Until you run out.

I came at it from another angle. I was a straight arrow in school. I drank a little in college, smoked some pot, so what. It didn't really ring my bell. But after I broke my back in a diving accident and the pain never went away, I discovered Vicodin. And when ten of them a day couldn't dull the knife jabbing in my spine and I was juggling three doctors to keep my prescriptions going, who just happened to show up at my physical therapy session? Jimmy Ortiz.

¤ ¤ ¤

My phone is barking at me. It's actually Vincent, the Lab from the TV show *Lost*. The display says my ex is calling.

What the hell. I've got a long drive ahead of me.

"Hello Allison." On my right, the lovely sight of the Long Beach refinery.

"Charlie..." She's crying. This is the sweet, remorseful Allison. She's going to try to reel me in. "I'm not your enemy."

"I know that, Allison. We've got to be on the same side..."

"And do what's best for Mindy," she sobs.

"Right. What's best for Mindy."

"I worry about her all the time." Her voice is low and husky. My guess is that she passed out in the late afternoon and is now on her third drink after waking up. She's in the sweet spot—the eight minutes where it's working for her. The rest is all about chasing the eight minutes.

"Have you heard from her yet?"

"No, I was hoping you had."

"She texted me a while back. I think she has a new boyfriend." I'm improvising, but the seeds that get planted now will surely bloom when Allison gets to crazyville.

"Really, have you met him?" I can hear the tinkle of ice on glass. She likes flavored vodka on the rocks.

"As a matter of fact, I have." This could get tricky.

"Really? What's he like?"

"Well, he seems to really like her."

"Why that little bitch." But this is purred, not hissed. "Tell her to call her mother, would you?" Her eight minutes are nearly over, and I have a chance to duck out before I have to duck for cover.

"I'll definitely do that, Alli. Listen, I'm driving and don't want to get a ticket. I'll have her call you soon."

"You do that, Charlie. Hey, are you anywhere nearby?" Oh boy. I've actually fallen for this one before. Lots of times. It's at least as dangerous as hooking up with Tanya.

"No, Alli, I'm actually down near Palos Verdes right now. I'm on a case." Finally, a true statement.

"Okay, that's too baa-ad," she says in a singsong voice. Accompanied by more tinkling of ice. Time to go.

"Bye Alli." I toss the phone on the seat next to me.

¤ ¤ ¤

A new vision unfolds. The memory doors seem to pop open at random. This is fifteen years ago and Mindy's a baby. Allison and I are on the couch in the living room of our starter condo in Culver City. Mindy's asleep and we're exhausted. Alli's leaning against me; I've got my arm around her, and all is right in a peaceful, quiet world. Then, like scene selections on a DVD, I'm getting images. No random selection, but a greatest-hits collection of every petty argument and cop-out and bullshit story that led to the war that our marriage became. And always the attempts to put it back together.

We hit rock bottom when Mindy was twelve. A marriage counselor suggested we take a trip. We left Mindy with Allison's sister in Sherman Oaks and found a bed-and-breakfast in La Jolla. The place was charming and the wine at dinner just right, and somehow Alli was able to let go enough to let me back in. We talked over dessert like we were on our third date. We reminisced and flirted and held hands and her toes crawled up my leg under the table. We made love that night and again in the morning.

That next day we planned a beach trip. We found an upscale market and bought French bread, soft cheese, smoked ham, black olives, and two bottles of wine, then drove to the beach. We ate and drank and baked in the sand. We held hands when we waded into the warm Pacific, then splashed each other and laughed till we fell down in the shallow surf. When we got back to our towels, we opened the second bottle of wine.

Somehow we wound up in the car, sandy and itchy from dried salt, our bathing suits still wet. We were arguing about something—how to get back to the bed-and-breakfast, I think—when we got to the cliffs. We were both more than half in the bag, but Allison seemed to have more tolerance for it than I did. The next thing I remember is standing with a bunch of teenagers and looking thirty feet down at the ocean. The kids jumped. Allison said, "Don't," and I dove, flying toward crystal clear blue-green water.

And that was the beginning of the nightmare. Ambulance, hospital, neck brace, doctor visits, pain meds, physical therapy, and, finally, Jimmy Ortiz and heroin.

¤ ¤ ¤

Time passes and I don't know where it goes. I check my phone and it tells me that I talked to Allison at 8:42. It's 10:15 now; I'm driving past the San Onofre power plant and have no recollection of the last hour and a half. I remember remembering something—diving off a cliff and hurting my neck—but something about it doesn't feel right. I call Allison. I know the timing is bad, but I've got to check on something.

"Taking me up on my offer? You're too late and a dollar short, you bastard..." Slurring and sloppy, spoiling for a fight, and I'm dumb enough to make myself a target.

"Alli, listen, I've got a question."

"Yeah, well the answer is fuck you. Ha! Yeah, fuck you, you sad little junkie loser."

It seems hopeless to expect her vodka-soaked brain to dredge up what I need, but I press on. "You're right," I tell her, "I'm a pathetic strung-out loser. You've always been right. About everything. Now, what happened when we went to La Jolla?"

"What happened? You mean how did you fuck up a perfectly nice holiday?"

"Sure, how did I fuck up our perfectly nice holiday?"

"You got drunk and jumped off a goddamn cliff. That's how you fucked up our holiday."

"Then what happened?"

"Jesus, you are pathetic. You got a two-hundred-and-fifty-dollar fine for ignoring the sign that said no diving. All those kids that dove in scattered, but the lifeguards caught you. Then we got a sixty-dollar parking ticket and you puked in the car. Any other questions?" She laughs into the phone and something falls with a loud thump in the background.

"Yeah, my back. How did I hurt it?"

"Boy, you really are an idiot. You flew headfirst over the handlebars of your bike. Do you remember your own name? Do you remember how much money you owe me?" Her voice is rising in volume and pitch now. "DO YOU REMEMBER WHAT YOU PUT ME THROUGH?"

I click the phone shut. My suspicion was correct and I'm in trouble. If I can't trust my memory, what can I trust?

At least I got the flying part right.

¤ ¤ ¤

I fly through Oceanside, Carlsbad, Encinitas, Del Mar. If my brain's a computer, it's in crash mode and needs to boot up from a new disk. Trouble is, I don't have a new disk. I'm stuck in a loop: morgue, Daniel, Jimmy's, Tanya, Ratboy, Mindy, jail, Jason. A gold mine and a silver Mustang. Did I make any of them up? And how do they all tie together?

I'm waiting in line at the border and my phone barks. Tanya asks me if I saw Jason. I tell her, "Yeah, we had a nice long talk."

"Well, did he tell you where my money is?"

"Yeah, he told me it's in the ground." *He was about to tell me more, but I was desperate to find Mindy, and Jason was dying.* For some reason, I withhold this information.

Tanya says, "That's just geo-speak for unmined gold— money in the ground. It's bullshit, as you know by now if you've read the report."

I've read two reports and they say opposite things, and I have no idea which one is correct, but why mention it?

"So where are you now, Charlie? Why don't you come back to the Oceana and we'll figure out what to do next?" It's the nice Tanya that's come out to play, which is about as reliable as the nice Allison.

"I don't think so, Tanya. I'm more concerned about finding my daughter than I am about your money." I click off just as a border guard waves me through. A chime tells me I have a new text message. It's from Allison, saying she still loves me.

Chapter 20

I've got the Z doing eighty down the toll road, past Ensenada. I should be coming up to San Vicente, the last town on the map before I go off the grid and onto dirt roads, into the mountains, flying blind. I want to crank it up to a hundred, climb on the roof, and howl at the moon, but there is no moon and the Z coughs and stutters in the darkness. It loses speed, and flooring the pedal doesn't help. The gas gauge says I have half a tank, so something is seriously wrong. Now we're chugging along at about twenty miles an hour. There's smoke billowing out behind me. The Z is a perfect metaphor for my life, lurching forward into barely illuminated gloom, the rear view a murky nothingness. A metallic bang signals the end, and I'm coasting, the sudden silence as big as the pitch-black sky.

The Z rolls to a stop on the side of the toll road. I turn the key off and kill the lights. Ensenada is far behind me. I haven't seen a car or an electric light in almost half an hour.

On a hunch, I pull out Jason Hamel's phone. It's down to one bar, but it's got GPS and I am thirty-eight miles south of Ensenada, with eight miles to go before I get to San Vicente. If I had a plan, it's changed, but it never included sitting in a dead car until something happened.

I grab Mo's gun from under my seat, along with DeShaun's. It's a Ruger .380 semi-auto, actually a pretty handy backup piece, if I need one. I step out of the Z and tuck the Ruger under my belt, up against the small of my back. Mo's 9 goes in front, enough to the side that my jacket covers it. I pocket all three cell phones and say good-bye to the Z. No way will it be there in the morning.

¤ ¤ ¤

The Z was my divorce present to myself. Actually, it was all I could afford after turning in the Lexus I could no longer make payments on. It was a red 1978 Datsun 280Z, the last of its kind, and it's been my friend for the past three years. Now it's road kill, carrion for scavengers who at best will leave a wheel-less frame on the side of the road.

I start walking in the dark.

My mind wanders.

There's something wrong with the whole picture from the start. Tanya used me as an intermediary in a blackmail scheme. She wanted to recover her husband's investment and keep it for herself. Jason Hamel wanted to destroy a report that would demolish his dream of a huge gold discovery and the Christian ministry that it would finance. The Caffeys were just about to publish their drilling results and were "very excited," according to James Caffey's widow. So why did they produce a report saying the mine has no value? And how did Tanya get both reports?

A memory.

¤ ¤ ¤

My first experience with heroin. I was at my physical therapy session. Two Hydrocodone tabs usually made PT tolerable, but this time they were useless. I sat in the waiting room with my head in my hands; I knew I couldn't go through with the session. I must have groaned or something, because this huge guy in the seat across from me said, "That bad, huh?"

I shook my head and said, "It gets like this once in a while."

He said, "Yeah, I know what you mean. I was eating Vicodin like candy."

And we were off and running, swapping stories about how we got hurt, how bad it was, how you can't crap on Vicodin and how not crapping gives you killer headaches. Finally, Jimmy said, "Yeah, it got to where I couldn't stand it anymore."

His use of the past tense got my attention. I asked him what he meant and he nodded toward the door. We got up and went out to the hallway to the men's room.

At this point, my new friend Jimmy Ortiz changed my life. I would get pain management at the cost of being tethered to heroin maintenance like a dog on a choke-chain: try to pull away, feel the pain.

Jimmy reached in his coat pocket and pulled out an amber vial with a black screw-on cap. From his jeans pocket he produced a mini Swiss Army knife. I watched, mesmerized, as he unscrewed the cap, dipped the tip of his blade into the vial, pulled out a tiny mound of white powder, and brought it to his nostril. A discreet whiff and the white powder disappeared.

Then it was my turn.

¤ ¤ ¤

I wonder what would happen if I left the body and just roamed into the night, as far from here as possible. What limit is there? Is it like there's an elastic cord that stretches thinner and thinner until it snaps? And then what? Didn't

Daniel tell me not to leave my body for too long? What's too long? I think I've pushed the limit a couple of times, and I didn't like the feeling.

A sound from behind. I keep walking. Now I'm casting a shadow, and the highway becomes visible as I trudge toward nowhere. A dirty, rusted pickup pulls up next to me.

"Hey, that your 280 back there?" It's a guy with long dirty hair, American. There's a blonde in the car with him. I show some teeth to signal that I'm friendly.

"Yeah. So far, anyway." I don't know how long I've been walking. The only reason the car is still there is that no one has seen it yet. Until now.

"Where'ya headed?" The blonde's teeth aren't so great, but she shows them all anyway. Signaling that she's friendly too, I suppose.

"San Vicente."

"Reservations at the Hilton?" They both start cackling. I don't like it.

I shrug.

"Well hey," the guy says. "You're fucked out here, so hop in." The blonde opens the door and slides toward the driver. I slide in and shut the door.

"Your car'll be gone in the morning." The guy's chewing gum like his life depends on it. The index finger of his left hand is wrapped in gauze and duct tape. He has a beer between his legs, and now he takes a swig from it and offers it to the blonde.

"Not much I can do about it."

"I don't know what your plans are in San Vicente, but you might be better off staying with us for the night. The town's shut down for the evening and there's nothin' there anyway. We got a place right up here a ways…" He gestures off into the darkness.

The blonde is tapping Heavy Metal rhythms with her fingers on her knee and bobbing her head like a pigeon. I consider my options, a speedy operation, like dividing a number by zero on a calculator: the answer is always "error."

"I'd appreciate that," I hear myself saying. But I know crazy when I see it.

The driver says, "Right on," and fishes a joint out of his pocket. He fires it up and passes it to me, sputtering, "Name's Herbie. This is Melinda. We got a place not far from here. It's your lucky night, pardner."

I take a hit off the joint just to be friendly, and say, "Charlie Miner."

Herbie and Melinda laugh their cackling laugh and Herbie stomps on the accelerator. The pickup lurches forward with astonishing power and veers left onto a dirt road that I didn't even see coming. Herbie turns off his headlights and we hurtle into oblivion with a roar, shaking and bouncing and kicking up rocks that hammer the undercarriage like a hailstorm.

Melinda takes the joint from me and hits on it like it's going to save her life. We hit something soft and bump over it, then a rise that sends us airborne. Herbie yells, "That's what I'm talkin' 'bout, motherfucker!" He finally slows down and turns the headlights back on. We turn left again, this time onto a narrow track between clusters of bushes that scrape the side of the truck. The path snakes around and uphill for a few minutes and we come to a stop at a gate. It's a crude contraption of two-by-fours and chickenwire, with barbed wire on top. In the glare of the headlights, I can see a level clearing butting up to the side of a cliff. There's a wooden shack on the left and, maybe twenty yards away, an RV on the right. In between, there's a recent-model Saturn with California plates.

Herbie gets out of the truck, saying, "Home sweet home," and opens the gate. He reaches in the back of the truck and pulls out a backpack, which he slings over his shoulder. Melinda scoots over and drives the truck in. She parks and gets out, taking a big flashlight from the glove box.

Herbie catches up with us and, guided by the beam of the flashlight, we go to the back of the shack. Herbie opens the door to a shed and starts the generator inside; it's a new, expensive-looking one that purrs as the lights go on in the shack. He goes back to the truck and gets a plastic cooler out of the back.

We go into home-sweet-home. Two lamps with ridiculous dried spiny blowfish shades show me a room about twenty feet square. It's got a concrete floor, but there's a sofa and a table with three chairs. To the left, there's a doorway to a dark hall. Straight ahead, there's a work bench with a laptop and a printer. An ice chest, a hot plate, and a microwave define the kitchen area to the right. Next to the ice chest, there's a rusted U-bolt sticking out of the concrete.

I'm standing looking at the room when suddenly there's an arm around my neck. I arch my back so Herbie won't feel the Ruger. Melinda pats me down and finds Mo's 9.

"Hey, whatcha got here? Well lookie, lookie." She checks the slide like a pro and puts the gun to my head. She's working her lips over her teeth in a weird way and her eyes have the demented look of a kid about to set a cat on fire.

I know she'd love to shoot me, but Herbie says, "Hey, stay cool," and she backs off. Herbie takes the gun from her and says, "Check it out! A P38-K. Always wanted one of these. Why, thank you, Charlie Miner." He winks at me. He's got a three-day beard, a soul-patch, and teeth as bad as his girlfriend's.

Melinda takes the phones out of my pockets and puts them on the table. She opens a drawer under the table and pulls out a pair of handcuffs. Herbie puts the barrel of the gun up to my right nostril and pushes me toward the ice chest. I stumble backward and land sitting on the floor.

"Get comfy, Charlie. It's gonna be a long night." Now he's got the gun pointed down at the top of my head. Melinda slaps one ring of the cuffs onto my left wrist and attaches the other to the U-bolt. I lean back against the wall, the Ruger safe behind me. I wonder how this is going to play out.

Chapter 21

Herbie takes the flashlight and steps outside while Melinda disappears through the hallway. I check out of the body and follow Herbie to the trailer. Inside is the meth lab from hell, a jungle of glassware and vats of solvents and reagents, open pizza boxes with half-eaten pizza slices, empty bottles of Jack Daniels, a fire extinguisher, and a Tec-9 semi-auto pistol. Next to the Tec-9 is a manual for conversion to full auto.

Herbie shines his beam on a six-inch glass tube half-full of shiny white crystals. He grabs the tube and heads back to the main house.

"Hey, wake up!" Melinda slaps me in the face just as I re-enter the body. I want to break her wrist, but now's not the time. My ex-wife was a slapper, my mother had a right hand like a cobra, and I feel a fury in my gut every time I see a slap in a movie.

Herbie comes back in and empties the contents of the plastic cooler—ice and cans of Coke and bottles of beer—into the ice chest. He looks down at me and laughs while he does it. He tosses the cooler aside and goes to the table. There's a glass pipe and a butane torch there, and Melinda's pacing around the table and chewing on the inside of her cheek.

"Sit the fuck down, Mel," Herbie commands, and she does, staring at the pipe like a dog waiting to be fed. Herbie pulls the rubber stopper off the vial and shakes some of the crystal into the bowl of the pipe. He fires up the butane torch and it looks like Melinda's going to bark like a trained seal.

Somewhere within ten miles of where I'm sitting, my daughter is being held captive by a psychotic untethered from any of the restraints that bind us to the social contract. The only thing on my side is that he's expecting his father to arrive. I notice that none of the cell phones have rung; for once it's helpful to be out of service range.

I expect the meth to get Herbie and Melinda even more agitated, but instead it seems to calm them down. Herbie comes over to me and kneels. "It's gonna be okay," he says. "We got a plan for you." He opens the ice chest next to me and pulls out a bottle of Jack Daniels. "So what's with the gun, matey?"

So now he's a pirate. Close to the truth seems as good as any story I could make up, so I tell him, "My daughter got kidnapped by her psycho boyfriend. I'm here to get her back. That's what the gun is for." Herbie's face is inches from mine, his breath an unpleasant mix of gum rot, cigarettes, and something metallic. It's the olfactory equivalent of chewing on tin foil.

"So how are you gonna find her down here?"

"She's at a mine. It's called Santa Clarita. Should be right near here."

"Yep. If we'd kept going instead of turning left we'd 'a wound up there. End of the road, can't miss it. Place is a fuckin' dump."

We're nose to nose now. I wonder if I could get the gun out and shoot them both, but I'm not feeling it. Instead, I say, "I'll pay you to let me go. Really. I'm desperate."

"Well, bum trip, Lone Ranger, your mission's gonna have to wait." I've seen the look in his eyes before, the glint of madness barely restrained, a hint of delight at the mayhem to come. He gets up and disappears into wherever the dark hallway goes.

When he comes back, he's got a four-foot rod with a white sheet furled around it. He opens the backpack and pulls out a digital camera. Melinda's fondling Mo's gun but puts it down when Herbie hands her the rod with the sheet. She unrolls it and tells me to lean forward, then she hangs it on the wall behind me.

Herbie's crouching in front of me now, aiming the camera at me. "Okay, smile," he says, and when I don't he says, "Okay don't, whatever," and clicks away. The flash goes off five times. After each flash he looks at the back of the camera and shakes his head. "You look like shit, dude," he says, and he gets up and takes the memory card out of the camera before putting it back in the pack.

Now Herbie goes to the workbench and fires up the printer and the laptop. He inserts the memory card into the laptop's port and uploads the photos. I watch as Photoshop loads and he sizes the images, then saves them and hits Print.

"That Blackberry on the table's got Global Positioning. The guys I hired to help me are within fifteen miles of here, and pretty soon they'll find me." It's worth a try.

Herbie steps over to where I'm sitting and his boot lashes out between my legs, catching me square in the huevos. I clamp my knees together and trap his foot, then I roll to my side. Herbie goes down and Melinda's got the gun in my face in a heartbeat.

Herbie gets up and brushes himself off. "You'll fuckin' pay for that, that's a fuckin' promise. But first you're gonna make a delivery." He hobbles over to the workbench and says, "Fuck! I think I got a sprained ankle."

I look up at Melinda. She wants to shoot me. There's something in her that wants to take this all the way, commit an irrevocable act, and seal the deal with her demons. Maybe she's done it before, but I don't think so; there's a war going on in Melinda's head. I tell her, "Hey, I've got a delivery to make," and she backs off and sits at the table. I watch her chew on her cheeks and fidget. The adrenaline must be messing with her high. She tilts the bottle of Jack and drains about a quarter of it and then smacks me in the head with the butt of the gun.

It's a good excuse to zone out. I play unconscious for a while, but all I hear is the butane torch hissing, the crackling of the meth in the bowl of the pipe, a cough, a long exhalation, and what sounds strangely like a sob.

Chapter 22

I leave the body and roam over to where Herbie's working. He has two photos of me, an X-acto blade, a US
passport, and a California driver's license. He's done
this before; his hands are steady and his work is pretty
good. I'm beginning to get a sense of his plan for me, but
still don't know how it works. I go back to my body.

"Didn't need to hit him like that," Herbie says.

"It won't show, so what's your problem?" Melinda's
got her high back. I hear the bottle of Jack thump down on
the table.

"I just decided to kill two birds with one stone," Herbie says. I hear a match flare and smell weed burning.

"How's that?"

"After delivery, I'm gonna send him to Mario's. When
Mario opens his front door, Ka-Boom! Goodbye fuckin'
deadbeat. He'll never pay us anyway."

I discover that I can watch without leaving the body
and without opening its eyes. My roaming body can just
sit there and observe and listen. Being dead is just full of
surprises.

Herbie crosses to stand behind Melinda and takes her
hair in his hand. She turns her head and accepts a lungful
of smoke; their lips lock in a lingering kiss—tweaker love
at its most poignant. Herbie sits down and starts with the
pipe and torch again.

I roam through the hallway into the back room. There's a mattress on the floor and a single lamp next to it on a board supported by two cinderblocks. Next to the lamp is a framed photo of Herbie and Melinda in better days. They're standing on the beach by a pier; Herbie in board shorts, tan and muscular, and Melinda looking hot in a skimpy bathing suit. They look happy.

There's a pile of clothes at the end of the bed, otherwise nothing in the room tells me anything useful. I go back to the body.

Junkies and tweakers are different breeds. They're looking for opposite effects: one wants to feel less and the other wants to feel more. They both wind up numb to everything except for the desperate need to continue staying numb. And so, they're different but the same. After all, addiction is addiction.

Herbie starts unwrapping the bandaging on his finger. Melinda says, "Christ, Herbie, you gotta stop that," but he ignores her. Now he reaches in his backpack and pulls out a magnifying glass on a metal base, the kind hobbyists use for close-up work, and sets it on the table. Next, he finds a scalpel, a needle, a bottle of alcohol, and a small amber vial.

"Herbie, the doctor said there's no glass in the cut. You gotta let it heal."

"Fuckin' beaner doctors don't know shit." Herbie uses the torch to sterilize the scalpel and the needle, then puts his hand under the magnifying glass. He pours a drop of Jack Daniels on the injured finger and shakes some powder out of the vial onto the cut.

"At least give me some of that," Melinda says. She takes the vial and empties half of it onto the top of her fist, then snorts the whole pile. "You're fuckin' wasting good coke."

"Shut up Mel. Just stop fuckin' ragging on me for five fuckin' minutes." Now he positions the flashlight so the beam is on his finger. He bends to the magnifier and goes to work with the needle. "How 'bout you set him up with the cuff."

"Fuckin' great." Melinda digs in the drawer and pulls out a shiny black plastic device. It looks like the lower half of a hinged knee brace, but with some modifications. There's a pocket inside, and a metal hasp on the outside. Melinda inserts a duct-taped package into the pocket; it's got an LED peeking out the top and a wire—probably an antenna—wrapped around it. Then she hikes my left pant leg up to my knee and puts the device on my ankle. She closes the hasp and secures it with a small three-ring combination lock. She goes to the table and pulls a transmitter out of the drawer; when she pushes a switch, the LED turns on. She puts the transmitter down and starts with the pipe and butane torch again.

¤ ¤ ¤

It's getting light outside. Herbie and Melinda have been getting high and arguing about his hand and the glass that is or isn't still in it. They've been talking about politics and their parents and which band is better, Metallica or AC/DC. They've been jabbering about getting clean and going to the Big Island. I can't stand it anymore so I decide to stir, making like I'm groggy and just coming to, which isn't far from the truth as roaming seems to take more out of me each time I try it.

"Hey, hey, the Lone Ranger's waking up." Herbie's smoking another joint and drinking a can of Coke, probably to keep his blood sugar up enough to fool his body into thinking it's being fed. "You messed up my ankle, dude, but I forgive you. I shouldn't have kicked you like that. My bad." He's hobbling around the table, circling it over and over, gesticulating with his arms spread wide. Melinda has her elbow on the table and her head propped up, cheek to hand.

"So what's the plan, Herbie?" He's squinting against the sunlight filtering through the dusty window.

"Charlie wants to know what the plan is. Melinda, why don't you lay it on him?"

Melinda's crashing. She looks at me without moving; her lips are chapped and the first two times she opens her mouth nothing comes out. I notice that the glass tube on the table is empty. She speaks in a monotone: "You've got a packet of C-4 explosive locked onto your leg. It's armed and ready to blow if I hit this button on the transmitter." Now she picks up the transmitter and shows it to me.

"It's got a range of two miles. If you get out of range, the loss of contact will detonate the explosive. If you try to take it off, it'll blow. If you detour from the plan, I hit the button and you're beef jerky."

"Okay, I got it. But what's the plan?" I'm guessing that I'm going to be a drug mule, but I want it spelled out by one of these bozos.

"You're just gonna get in the car and drive back to the States. As soon as you're across the border in San Ysidro, you're pulling into the Denny's on your right and swapping cars with Herbie. You'll have one more quick job to do and we'll disarm the detonator and text you the combination to the lock." The right corner of her lip edges up in a weird parody of a smile.

"What about my daughter?"

Herbie says, "Not our problem, man. Maybe the team you're supposed meet up with will save the day." He laughs as he opens the door and goes outside, putting on sunglasses as he goes.

"He's actually a really good guy," says Melinda. "This is our last run and then we're moving to Kona. We're gonna get clean and just grow weed."

"That's good, Melinda. That's really good. Maybe I can visit someday."

She looks almost sad for a moment. "I don't think that's gonna happen, Charlie."

Herbie comes back in with a backpack. He puts it on the table and pulls out three packages. Each one is about the size of a brick and is wrapped securely with duct tape. Where the tape isn't covering it, I can see a brick of white powder wrapped in clear plastic. Herbie's been a very busy little cook.

"Okay Charlie, from now until we meet up north, you're Paul Cleary." He tosses the passport and driver's license on the floor in front of me. He turns to Melinda and says, "I'm gonna go into town and gas up the car. Then I'll take care of the plates and put the product in the doors."

Melinda doesn't look happy. She's got shades on too; she's fidgety and the Jack Daniels bottle is empty. "Aren't you gonna leave me a little something?"

She's whining now and Herbie doesn't like it. "Stay focused, Mel. When I'm back I'll fix you up. It's just fuckin' town and back, twenty minutes, fuckin' live with it."

And he leaves.

¤ ¤ ¤

I watch Melinda deteriorate over the next five minutes. She gets up and paces, sits down and drums her fingers on the table, chews on her cheek, and keeps a separate drum beat with her left knee vibrating the table.

For fun, I say, "Hey, can I get up and go to the bathroom? I've been sitting here for hours."

She jumps up like a startled rabbit and yells, "Shut the fuck up." She has the transmitter in her hand and thrusts it at me like a knife fighter. She puts it on the table and circles it, staring at the bricks of meth. Finally, she pulls a knife out of the drawer and opens a corner of one of the bricks. She pulls a chunk of the powder out and drops it in the glass pipe and sits down and starts the butane torch.

She's staring at the bowl of the pipe as the heat hits the powder and it starts turning into a gas when I pull out DeShaun's Ruger. I shoot her in the left knee. The pipe flies out of her hand and the torch drops to the table, hissing as it spits a thin blue flame. I aim the Ruger at Melinda's face. "Hands up. Very slowly, I want you to give me the key to the handcuffs."

Her hands go up. The transmitter is right in front of her.

"I don't have them. They're in the other room. I can't walk."

I aim at her other knee and say, "Counting, one, two..."

She says, "Okay, okay, they're right here." She reaches into the drawer. If she pulls out a gun, I'm in trouble since I'll have to shoot her and start all over again with Herbie. I aim at her face again and repeat, "Slow, Melinda, really slow and careful."

Her hand comes out with the key. I tell her, "Good. Now, lean toward me and toss the key right here." I gesture to the floor in front of me. She's only five feet away, but she's messed up, and the key could fly like the pipe did.

The key lands on the concrete at my feet.

I keep the gun pointed right between her eyes. "Hey, Melinda..."

"What?" She's in shock, which is useful because it's keeping her calm.

"Hands behind your head ... that's good. Now, use your right foot, push yourself away from the table... good, farther. Okay, stay like that." She's far enough from the transmitter that she can't get to it. I have a feeling there's enough C-4 on me to blow us both up and she knows it, but she could be crazy enough to take us both out.

I keep the gun on her while I open the cuff on my wrist. I get up and take Melinda by the elbow and help her up.

"What are you doing? I can't walk."

I pull on her elbow and she starts to keel over. She's about five eight but couldn't weigh more than a hundred pounds. I lower her to a sitting position and drag her to where I had been all night and bang the cuff on her wrist. It goes to its smallest diameter before it's snug enough to keep her from slipping her hand out.

The butane torch is starting to scorch the table. I turn it off and sit in the chair Melinda was just in. There's blood on the floor. I scoot over so that I'm right in front of her and say, "Okay, now, stay with me. If you get this right, I'll bring you the pipe and the torch and a whole damned brick, okay?"

She nods, wild-eyed, starting to shiver. She's holding her leg with her free hand and rocking back and forth.

"The combination, Mel. I need the combination."

"Three-eight-six," She says in a croaking stammer.

I slide the chair back to the table and pick up the transmitter. I lift my pant leg up to expose the device; the red LED is visible. I flick off the "Arm" switch on the transmitter and the LED winks out. The combination is good and the whole thing comes off.

On a hunch, I take it outside and go into the trailer. There's a ten-gallon drum of benzene on the workbench. I take the C-4 packet and radio detonator out of the ankle cuff and put it behind the drum.

Melinda's shaking now. I retrieve the pipe from the floor; it's broken and useless. I hold it up to show her and she nods toward the table. I open the drawer—it's deep and compartmentalized—and find another pipe. I hand it to Melinda, along with the torch and the already opened brick.

¤ ¤ ¤

I go outside again. The gate is closed and the dirt road extends downhill through about a mile of brush. I can see the juncture to the main road that leads to the highway. The truck is parked right next to the house; the trailer is about fifty feet away. Behind it, the hills rise steeply, sparse and rocky.

Back in the house, Melinda's lying on one side, propped on her elbow so she can use her cuffed hand to hold the pipe while she aims the torch with her right. Blood is drying, dark brown and stiff, on her jeans. She lets out a cloud of smoke.

"So what are you gonna do when Herbie gets back?"

"Guess I'm going to have to shoot him. Got any better ideas?"

"You could make a deal with him. You can take the car and leave. No problem. Just don't shoot him."

I think about the photo of them in the other room. Somewhere in their feeble minds they still think of themselves as the couple in the picture.

"He's planning on killing me after I finish my delivery."

Melinda goes wide-eyed on me. "No, man, that's not true, he wouldn't do that."

"Two birds with one stone. Mario. Ka-Boom. I heard the whole plan."

"He was just high. He talks out of his ass when he's like that, for real."

I go back to the drawer and rummage through it. There's a plastic shopping bag in one of the compartments. It's got an extra pack of C-4 and a remote. There's a high-intensity flashlight and a pair of binoculars. I'm thinking if I get out of here and actually make it up the hill to the mine, this stuff could be useful. I wrap the pack of C-4 in a rag and put everything in the backpack.

I crack the door and see the Saturn stop at the gate. Herbie gets out and swings it open. I back into the house and crouch in the hallway to the bedroom, aiming the Ruger at the door. Melinda sits up and stares at the door, the torch in her free hand spitting its flame into the air.

The door starts to open and I'm ready to fire. Melinda yells, "Herbie, run!" and throws the torch at me. My shot goes wild as the torch bounces off my shoulder.

I sprint for the door and catch Herbie running toward the trailer. I fire at him from behind the truck, but miss as he goes up the steps into the trailer. He turns and fires twice with Mo's gun; the rounds slam into the side of the truck as he opens the door and disappears inside.

I wait and watch. The Saturn is parked down the drive-way, washed-out blue as the bright and cloudless sky; crows circle overhead, flapping and cawing in the morning sun. The trailer's door starts to open. I put two bullets in it and it closes again.

Melinda's voice screams, "You're gonna die, mother-fucker," and a barrel pokes through the louvered windows on the side of the trailer. More bullets slam into the truck and fly past me in a swarm. I guess he got the Tec-9 con-verted to full auto. I fire at the windows and duck back into the house.

Melinda's staring at me triumphantly. "You're so fucked!"

I go straight to the table, pick up the transmitter and push the "Arm" switch. I tell Melinda, "Say goodbye to the Big Island." A clatter from the Tec-9 sends bullets through the thin wood wall of the house and out the other side. I push the red button.

¤ ¤ ¤

Melinda screams an endless "Noooo..." that is drowned out by the explosion. Debris clatters against the wall of the shack; seconds later, more lands on the roof. After a few minutes the crows return and Melinda's scream subsides to a convulsive sobbing.

The trailer's not looking too good. I hope the keys are in the Saturn, or I'm in for Freddy Krueger's Easter egg hunt. I duck back into the shack for the backpack. I sweep up the three cell phones and put them into the pack. For some reason I feel thirsty, so I grab a Coke out of the cooler. Melinda looks up at me and says, "What about me?"

"What about you, Melinda? Just a minute ago you were all excited about me getting killed, and now you want my sympathy?"

"You can't just leave me here like this."

"Well, yes I can. There's a cloud of black smoke a quarter mile high coming off the trailer. I'm sure somebody's going to be dropping by soon." I retrieve the torch and toss it to her. "Here, this'll keep you entertained." The flame is out.

"It needs butane." She's pathetic now, eyes pleading. She looks to the drawer.

I pull out a new can of butane and hand it to her.

"Bye, Melinda. It's been swell."

Chapter 23

ood news. The keys are in the Saturn and the tank
is full. I am now Paul Cleary; my driver's license
says so. And my passport. I've got a gun with a few
bullets, a mini-bomb with a remote detonator, a flashlight,
cell phones with no signal, and clear directions to the mine.

I feel strangely invigorated, and the cold coke tastes
good going down my throat. The dirt is brown and the
shrubs a dull green; I can see color, though it's washed out
and dim, like at dusk. I wonder if my condition is improv-
ing. Maybe I was just badly wounded.

Yeah, right. And whoever delivered me to the morgue
was an idiot. And besides, badly wounded wouldn't explain
my ability to leave the body. Roaming seems to be a special
privilege of some kind of extraordinary state.

Or I'm badly wounded and delusional. Now there's a
possibility.

There's a film I saw in college: During the Civil War,
a man is about to be hanged from a bridge. Union soldiers
are standing guard. The rope breaks and the man swims
down the river toward safety. Pursued by rifle shots and
baying hounds, he finds a road and runs toward his plan-
tation home. A beautiful woman seems to float down the
steps from the veranda, her hand stretched out to greet
him. When their fingers touch, the rope snaps taut and

the man is hanging from the bridge. There's a book about Jesus on the cross that's basically the same story. I wonder if that's my story too: to wake up and die.

I'm down Herbie's hill at the juncture of his private driveway and the road back to the highway. Left on that road takes me into the hills, to the mine.

To Ratboy.

To Mindy.

There's nobody in the world that I'm closer to than Mindy. She understands me with a wisdom that I can't begin to explain. She knows my problems and forgives me unconditionally. Her mother says it's because I let Mindy do whatever she wants, that Allison's been forced to play bad cop to my good cop for so long that in Mindy's eyes I can do no wrong, but I think there's more to it than that.

Well, I would, wouldn't I?

I make the left turn and head up into the hills. The road crosses a dry creek bed and gets steeper. I put the Saturn into second gear. I can see the plume of black smoke from the trailer over my left shoulder.

I'm high enough in the hills that I can see the ocean in the rearview mirror. The sun catches just right through the windshield and I'm blinded for a second. I hear another echo of the roaring in my head, the bullet invading my skull; I'm flying off the bike and there's a face behind the gun. Is it Ratboy's? Or his partner's? I can't capture it. What doesn't make sense is Ratboy showing up at the restaurant for the reports. Did Jason send him? Then who was Tanya talking to at the coffee shop when she said that I didn't show up with the briefcase? Her husband? Where does he fit in the picture? And why are there two conflicting reports?

The road crosses over the creek bed again and then goes parallel to it into a sort of dip between two hills. The brush is scraping the car on both sides, and the Saturn's shocks weren't built for this terrain. The road gets bumpier as it gets steeper. I wonder if the C-4 in the backpack is sensitive to jostling; I have no experience with it. Nor do I have experience with gun fights, gold mines, or the Mexican desert, but there's only one way to go and that's forward. Unless the C-4 turns me and the Saturn into a second pillar of black smoke in the Mexican sky.

I hit the top of a rise and the view changes entirely. The road leads down into a flat valley nestled between the hills, with higher terrain about a half mile on the other side. About twenty yards down from the top of the rise there's a partially open gate with barbed wire and a sign that says "Private Property." There's a stand of trees on either side of it. The barbed wire extends north and south from the gate. I decide to park in the shelter of the trees.

I grab the backpack and walk to the tree nearest the gate. The valley sits in a depression in the hills, about two hundred feet below me. To my left, the hill I'm on steep-ens and becomes an almost vertical wall forming the north side of the valley. Set against it is a long, rectangular con-crete building, its single door open. Two small shacks sit next to it. Beyond them is a water tank and then a series of pyramid-shaped mounds, some taller than the building. A bulldozer sits idly in the dirt. Cactus and mesquite trees grow randomly, some right up to the side of the structure. The road from the gate leads down to the building and then veers south and recedes into the distant hills. Down that road, about halfway to the building, is the Chevy van I saw in the picture in Ratboy's room.

Bingo.

It's a weird place to have stopped and parked. Herbie's binoculars bring the van up close, and I don't like what I see. First of all, the van seems to have veered partly off the road and is turned sideways to me. I sharpen the focus and see that the windshield is missing. I swap the binoculars for DeShaun's gun and sling the backpack over my shoulder. I head down the road, keeping the van between me and the concrete building.

The driver's side door is open. There's shattered glass all over the seats and floor, but no one inside, and no blood. I step in and crawl between the seats; the rear of the van is carpeted with thick plush. Aside from fast-food wrappers and some empty beer bottles, the only thing I see is a pair of Mindy's sunglasses, the same pair she was wearing when I picked her up forever ago at her mother's.

I run my hands through the plush, combing it with my fingers. Up against the bench that runs lengthwise behind the driver's seat, right at the juncture with the floor, I feel a hard, metallic nugget. It's a bullet, flattened from impact. A bit more scrabbling around yields two more. I study the passenger-side panel and see the light streaming in from three holes.

I could play it safe and roam, but last time the re-entry knocked me out for a while and left me disoriented, which wouldn't be good if anyone decided to check out the van. Instead, I slip back between the seats and crouch in front of the passenger seat and peer out the window. There's a body about thirty feet away, sprawled in the middle of the dirt road.

The van's door opens with a loud squeal. I drop to the ground and move, crab-like, toward the body. Something crunches under my hand; a tarantula's body fluids seep between my fingers and remind me of the blood flowing from Jason Hamel's wound.

A heavily tattooed Mexican wearing a wife-beater tucked neatly into baggie shorts lies on his back in the dirt. His head is shaved and has a red devil's face tattooed on it with Roman numerals on his forehead. He looks like he spent most of his life pumping iron. There's a pool of blood in the middle of his chest, and flies are buzzing over it. I get closer and see maggots squirming blindly on his neck and shoulders. There's a gun in his right hand, a big military issue S&W .45.

I kneel to remove the gun, as the Ruger is down to two bullets. A hand snaps out and grips my wrist. I see the gun swing around to point in my direction as the man's eyes pop open and glare at me. Our eyes meet and his expression turns from a triumphant leer to one of panic. He screams, "No, no, Madre de Dios, no," and coughs up blood. His body quivers, the gun fires over my shoulder, and his eyes lock in a stare to nowhere. The quick and the dead, two qualities that should never combine, and he saw them both in me. So, I am vindicated. At least the dying know what I am.

I take the gun, which has fallen out of the man's hand. A shot rings out and the dirt flies up three feet to my left. Another shot, this time slamming into the van's front hubcap and sending it spinning off into a cactus thicket. A third one hits me just under the right clavicle. I feel the impact, but no pain. I let it take me to the ground and lie spread-eagled and motionless. Leaving the body, I watch an older man walk up the road from the building, a rifle in his hand. He's dark and lean and has a face like a crumpled grocery bag. His denim shirt has mother-of-pearl snap buttons that match the huge buckle on his belt. His teeth are the color of the plug of tobacco he spits out as he raises the rifle.

I re-enter the body and fire into the man's heart. The rifle sounds like a cannon as it discharges five feet from my face, but the bullet hits the dirt beside me.

I will the body to move. I will the heart to pump the blood to feed the cells to imitate life. I'm getting better at this. My shoulder wound bleeds, but I go on.

¤ ¤ ¤

The gunshots don't seem to have attracted any more attention. I approach the building holding the dead man's rifle
in one hand, the .45 in the other. The windows are small
and square and about head high, but if I'm going to offer a
target to anyone inside, my face isn't my first choice, so I
duck through the door, ready to fire. There's no one inside.
It's all one room, about forty feet long and twenty wide.
Four bunk beds are in the far end, two against each of the
longer walls, with a couple of ramshackle chests of draw-
ers between them. I approach the beds; they have uncov-
ered mats on them and resemble the ones at the county
jail. Each has a sleeping bag rolled up at its end. There's no
sign that Mindy has been here.

The other end of the building has a huge table propped
up on two-by-fours. Workbenches line the walls, covered
with buckets of rock and dirt. There's a kitchen corner
with a steel sink and a hose for a faucet. A wooden chair
faces a mirror that is stuck to the wall. A four-burner electric hotplate and a small refrigerator, along with a few
hanging light bulbs, indicate that there must be a generator somewhere outside.

The big table is strewn with junk: buckets of dirt and
rock; magnifiers and an old microscope; various tongs and
long, needle-nosed tweezers; a hatchet and a fire extinguisher; a boom box and a stack of CDs—Marvin Gaye,
Quincy Jones, Aretha Franklin; a terrain map, presumably
of the mine and the surrounding mountains; and the odd
pen, flashlight, sunglass case, and pocketknife, all covered
with a layer of dust. It looks like someone left years ago,
planning on coming back the next day.

I go back outside. There's a broad expanse of nothing
but the occasional cactus or bush ahead of me. The dirt
road comes down from my right and then bears south—

the way I'm facing—to some hills miles away. To my left are the two shacks and the mounds of dirt, and, far beyond that, an incongruously wooded hill.

The shacks are empty. Bunks with mats. Rat shit on the window sills. They look like they were built by the same guy that made Herbie and Melinda's palace, but this time he was in more of a hurry. There's an outhouse past the second shack that I couldn't see before. Still no sign of Mindy or Ratboy and his giant friend.

I walk past the water tank, which has a Rube Goldberg set of PVC pipes leading back to the main building. Behind it, to my left, is the steep hill, almost a cliff, that backs the main building and the shacks. Ahead of me is the first of the dirt and rock mounds I viewed from the gate at the entrance. It's about twelve feet high, and I have to walk around it to the right or climb over the lower part that butts up against the cliff. I keep the rifle pointed ahead of me as I climb.

There's a hole in the cliff, just past the mound of dirt, about five feet high, with a scaffolding of two-by-fours propping it up at the opening. A wheelbarrow sits on its side in the shadows about five feet in. I sit with my back to the wheelbarrow, scan the valley for any sign of life, and leave the body. About ten feet into the tunnel I realize it's useless; I can't see in the dark any better than when I am in the body. I re-enter the body and put the rifle down and the backpack next to it. Herbie's flashlight and the dead Mexican's .45 point my way into the dark.

Chapter 24

I've always hated the dark, but enclosed spaces make my head want to explode. For our honeymoon, Allison and I went to Italy. It had always been a dream of hers to see the Vatican, the ruins of Pompeii, the Amalfi coastline, the tower in Pisa; we did it all, holding hands and exploring like high-school kids in love. One day we were having lunch in Siena when a middle-aged British couple sitting at the table next to ours started telling us about the bell tower of the church across the piazza from us. "Fabulous," the woman said. "You can see for miles in every direction."

After lunch, Allison and I walked to the church. A buck apiece bought us entrance to a narrow, winding stairway, just wide enough to let one person climb at a time. I went first. A tiny, dim bulb shaped like a candle and strung on a wire once at every full turn of the stairway provided just enough light to see the steps. The amber-colored walls were cool and smooth. About six turns up, the person ahead of me stopped; someone was descending and neither could pass. Allison was right behind me, with the British couple—on board for their second time—at her back. The lights flickered, became suddenly very bright, and then died with a faint clicking sound.

If I had been in a sarcophagus under a pyramid I would have been more comfortable. I wanted to go berserk, to push Allison and start a domino effect of fallen tourists I could trample on my way to open space. I got short of breath, dizzy and desperate, and prayed the prayer of the momentary believer: *Help me, I'll do anything.*

¤ ¤ ¤

And now, here I am, stooped over and shuffling into the narrow blackness, the beam from the light illuminating nothing but a small circle on the ground. I will the body to move. I trudge on, full of dread, ready to put a hole in the next tweaker, gangbanger, or Mexican thug that gets in the way of me finding my daughter. I aim the light ahead; it gets lost in the gloom. I walk face first into a spider web and want to scream and tear my skin off. I wipe my face in the crook of my arm and keep moving.

I must be forty feet into the tunnel. It's starting to veer to the left; when I pass the bend, the darkness is complete. It's quiet as a tomb. There's a beer bottle on the ground, and some loose chunks of rock, but if Mindy's in here she's either not awake or not alive.

The silence is broken by a sudden flutter of wings and a chorus of squeaking that I never want to hear again, followed by a weird shriek and hoof beats on the tunnel floor. A wave of bats flitter around my head and in the slender beam of the flashlight I see a beast charging at me. It looks like a hairy black pit bull with tusks for the tiny second I can see it before it slams into my legs and knocks me on my back. The flashlight goes out as it flies from my hand. The beast's hoofbeats recede into the darkness while the bats swirl above me in a sonic nightmare of leathery fluttering and squeals.

If it weren't for Mindy, I'd have given up long ago. I don't know what gods I've offended, but they're having their way with me now.

¤ ¤ ¤

Time goes by, who can measure? The bats have settled down; somewhere up above they're happily perched, upside down, grasping the rock ceiling with their claws, folded into their wings, back to their bat dreams. I seem to be indestructible, and yet I feel so vulnerable. Snakes like caves—I read that somewhere. Scorpions, spiders, poisonous lizards, guns with silencers, rat-faced killers, yes!—and rats, too, scurrying here where I've made my bed, it seems, for I've lost interest in moving.

I paw at the dirt on my right side until I feel the cool metal of the flashlight. I grasp it and hit it with heel of my left hand. Nothing. I push the button and remain in the dark. The batteries fall onto my chest when I unscrew the cap. I put them back in and the beam appears like a comet, slicing through pitch black like a laser through obsidian.

I sit up and swing the light around the tunnel walls and now the floor. No rats and not a snake in sight. I'm glad I left the backpack at the entrance; falling on the C-4 might have left me with too many separate parts to get moving again. I pick myself up and follow the beam back around the bend; the mouth of the tunnel is a circle of sunlight ahead of me.

The view of the desert is like a balm to the soul, space to move and breathe, the sun my friend, the sheltering sky. I tuck the .45 in my pants, put the flashlight in the backpack, and pick up the rifle. East, away from the tunnel and the mounds of dirt and the water tower and the buildings, away from the dead Mexicans and Ratboy's van and my nice new car, out toward the foothills and the patch of greenery I saw from the main building.

It's a weird little desert oasis, thick with mesquite and palms and, now that I'm closer, flowering sage. It fills a shallow canyon that cuts into the foothills and veers to my left in a gentle slope for about a quarter mile before tapering off into the surrounding hills.

I climb some boulders and find a worn path through the bushes. It winds through the trees and rocks and brings me to a stream that originates somewhere at the top of the canyon and bends to the south just ahead of me. I wade across and wind up on a sandy beach in the crook of the bend. Footprints are scattered everywhere, and the remains of a fire smolder in a small depression in the sand. I am in Ratboy's sacred place, the stream where his adoptive father baptized him.

Upstream, to the northeast, the bank to my left rises steeply, becoming a rock wall after about a hundred yards. On my side of the stream, the patch of sand narrows and becomes a muddy path between the water and a grade of boulders and dirt and bush. Two sets of footprints are clearly visible, one fairly small and terminating in a distinct point—I recall Ratboy's boots—and the other simply enormous, making huge gouges in the soft mud. I follow their lead, rifle ready. A hawk soars overhead and swoops down to my right, emerging from a crevasse between two giant rocks with something gray and furry wriggling in its talons.

The stream narrows and deepens. A cluster of boulders and trees make an island that interrupts the water's flow so that it quickens where it has cut a path to either side. As I approach I raise the rifle, since I can't see beyond the fork in the stream. Beyond it, the mud path disappears, along with the footprints. Standing there, upstream from the little island, I look at the opposite bank and see a rock spur jutting out from the cliff. It causes the water to churn before it meets the island and divides. In the crook on the downstream side of the spur is a depression in the cliff wall and a flat rock platform about a foot underwater leading into it.

I wade across to the island through waist-high water. A fallen tree gives me something to grab onto and I climb to the top of the largest rock. I am ten feet above the water, looking down at the depression in the cliff, and I can see now that it darkens as it recedes into the rock wall. It's a crevasse, deep in the shadows even now at midday. The swirling water looks deep on this side, but it's only about eight feet to the shallow rock shelf, and there's a lower boulder I can launch from.

I lay the rifle down and remove the backpack. The .45 and the flashlight will be my friends in the dark once again, if I make it past the mouth of the cave. I put them in the backpack and remove the C-4 and detonator and lay them on the rock and strap the pack on my shoulders. I climb down to the launch-point and study the water. There's no way to tell how deep it is, but it's moving and probably over my head. I hurl myself upstream and stroke across and am conveniently swept by the current onto the rock shelf.

I'm ankle-deep in water, but in three steps I'm inside of the rock wall, crouching in the dim light, waiting to be shot once again, the .45 ready in one hand and the flashlight, not yet on, in the other. Four more steps and I'm in total darkness, moving as silently as I can. I hear a clatter and shushing sounds coming from somewhere ahead of me. I freeze and hear the click of a hammer being cocked. I whisper loudly, "Jason!"

Silence. A rustling sound, then Ratboy's voice, incredulous: "Dad?"

I take three steps forward, four, five. I have no idea where they are. I whisper his name again: "Jason, where are you?"

Now his voice is desperate, grateful, pathetic. "Dad, I'm sorry. They took over the camp." The voice is coming from right in front of me. I say nothing. He blurts out, "Dad, is that you?" I turn on the flashlight: he's a deer caught in headlights; his left shoulder is bandaged and bleeding; his gun pointed randomly out to his right; his lazy eye blinks out of synch with the good one. I say, "Nope," and shoot him in the forehead.

A roar of pain and rage erupts from the shadows and Ratboy's gorilla-shaped friend charges at me. His unformed features make him look like a thug with a nylon stocking over his face, a giant, dumb bank-robber. He slams me into the rock wall and picks me up and throws me across the cave and charges again. I drop the flashlight as I hit the opposite wall, but this time it stays on. I leave the body and let it crumple to the ground.

From above, in the minimal glow of the flashlight, I can see Ratboy's body collapsed against the wall in a sitting position where the cave ends in a rounded cul-de-sac. Mindy lies curled up a few feet away, alive or dead I can't tell. I watch Gorilla-boy raise a fist and smash my face. He raises it again. I float to Ratboy and probe. I move closer; there's nothing in my way, and I move in. I look through Ratboy's eyes and raise his gun and pull the trigger. The first bullet hits Gorilla-boy in the ass but he delivers his blow anyway. I fire again, and again, and again. The monster falls over with a groan and stops moving.

¤ ¤ ¤

I exit Ratboy's body and linger in the dome of the cave space. I feel contaminated, soiled as though immersed in a psychic cesspool, infected by a soul-sickness one can only confront with dread, or with a faith larger than I've ever known. I hesitate to take this sickness back to my own body, as though it might take residence there like a stain that can never be washed away.

I re-enter my body because I have to. It's badly damaged, but serviceable. I put my hand to the back of my head; it's crushed from the impact against the cave wall and feels soft, like baby fat. My right cheek is smashed and I can feel bits of bone crunching when I press it with my fingers. I pick up the flashlight and go over to Mindy. She's inert but breathing, either drugged or knocked unconscious.

I go back to Ratboy's body and search his pockets. A rabbit's foot—but no, I check it out with the flashlight and it looks more like it once belonged to a cat; a folding combat knife; a wallet; and a small Ziploc baggie full of pills, but no keys. I have to struggle with Gorilla-boy's body to turn him over and get to his front pocket, where I find a set of keys and put them in my pocket. I shine the light on his face; he looks like a huge sleeping infant, all malice gone. Ratboy still looks like a rat, his expression frozen into a permanent sneer, his upper lip pulled back so that his canines glint wetly in the flashlight's beam.

I retrieve the .45 and tuck it in my pants. Mindy feels light as a feather as I pick her up, but is completely unresponsive. I stagger to the mouth of the cave and step down onto the submerged shelf and launch myself backward into the stream. The current carries us a short way until my feet touch bottom and I can walk to the opposite side and climb up the rocks to the mud path. I take Mindy back to the beach and lay her next to the fire pit and go back up the path, across to the island, and retrieve the C-4 and the rifle.

Mindy's still unconscious when I get back to her. I hoist her onto my back and head toward the sun. My vision is dim; the desert and sky look grainy and dark, even though it's still, by the sun's position, mid-afternoon. The trees and bushes are amorphous shapes, without definition or significance, and I know only that I have to get to the building and that in order to do that I have to keep the hillside to my right. I'm obsessed with two things: one is to get Mindy home to safety; the other is that someone set this all in motion, and I'm going to find out who and why.

Chapter 25

There is no time. There is only another step into shades of gray, and another, the sun a quicksilver plate in the sky. I will the body to move. I drop the rifle; it's useless to me now. I wear the backpack on my chest, my daughter on my back, my shoes squeak wetly. I trudge onward and try to retrieve the pieces to the puzzle. Tanya, the conflicting geologist's reports, Ratboy at the restaurant, riding my bike, the gun in the Mustang's window, waking up at the morgue. Jason senior and his obsession with gold. There is no thread of coherence to it all.

Mindy's hand twitches where it rests against my elbow. A good sign, I hope. A mound appears to my right, and a structure, a giant can on stilts. I struggle to put a name on it: *water tower*. I pass the two shacks and arrive at the main building. The body wants to quit. I've driven on fumes and flat tires to get where I needed to go, but now the wheels are coming off and we're not going to make it any farther. I fumble with the door and turn right and shuffle across the room to the nearest bunk, turn and sit and ease Mindy onto the mat, brush back her hair and stare. I am void of thought or feeling.

Her breathing is shallow but steady.

I find myself standing at the workbench, with no memory of walking to it, and no intention. There is light but it seems dark.

I'm sitting in the chair, facing the mirror. In my hand are the long-nosed tweezers from the work bench. I don't know why. I squint at my reflection and try to remember what I am looking at. For some reason, I'm sitting in a chair at the beach, across a card table from a man with closed eyes. He opens them and stares into mine and says, "Commune with your spirit to begin healing." The beach dissolves and I am staring into my own eyes, my ruined cheek sagging, my hair plastered to the dried dust on my forehead, blood caked from my nose to my upper lip.

I don't know anything about communing with my spirit. What I see is the enormity of my neglect, the denial, the procrastination, the hiding behind a haze of opiates; dishonesty, grasping selfishness, and isolation. It hits me with a clarity unthinkable just a moment ago: the fact of my pathetic condition even before Ratboy shot me. I am back on my bike, approaching my driveway, the silver Mustang creeping up behind me, the shot, the sting, the clattering of my bike and the impact of my head on the asphalt, and Ratboy's voice: "Fuck you, turkey." The roaring begins.

As the Mustang drives off, a shape appears against the night sky. It's triangular, like a giant stingray, dark as the space between the stars. It spirals down from above me. The roaring sound intensifies. It obliterates everything else; sound, sight, and sensation are subsumed into the tornado, at the center of which is a weird peace.

And now a new memory, the next part of the sequence. Underneath the roaring I can hear a calm, informative voice delivering instructions like a CNN reporter reading off stock quotes. It seems to be telling me the rules of my new condition, but because of the hurricane I can't decipher every word. I barely make out something about "re-integration with and repair of the body... retribution is allowed" and "killing of innocents... permanent dissolution." I wonder about that phrase, permanent dissolution. How bad can that be, really? Isn't that what Buddhist meditation is about? Isn't that what every junky is looking for? And who is an innocent, anyway?

The shape hovers and recedes. The roaring subsides. I hear police sirens and see flashing red and blue lights. And then, oblivion.

I turn my head to the right and with the index and ring fingers of my right hand part the hair and spread the bullet wound. The hole is a little over a quarter inch in diameter. With my left hand I slide the tweezers in. They're eight inches long and go halfway in with no resistance. I poke slightly upward, trying to feel for the metallic resistance of a bullet and...

I'm poolside in Palm Springs, drinking an ice cold Dr. Pepper. It's spring break and I'm seventeen. My skin is wet, the sun is fierce, and voices are chattering around me. The part of me that's dreaming pulls back on the tweezers and I'm back in the wooden chair.

I try again. No bullet. I move the steel points slightly to the left. I'm sitting on my father's shoulders, staring face to face at an ape in a zoo enclosure. He's only eight feet away. He reaches a black hand toward me. My hand moves and I'm looking in the mirror.

One more try. This time I poke downward. My left-hand coordination isn't great at the best of times, which doesn't include right now. Once more I'm transported, this time to only a week ago, picking through apples at the Safeway. The sensation is so real I can feel the texture of the fruit. I wish I could go back to the first time I had sex with Joanie Bennett in college, but now's not the time.

I once read an article about how memories are stored in the brain, and that every moment is stored holograph-ically in the cells but that there's no map or indexing sys-tem for finding a specific image or experience.

I have another idea. I lean back and leave the body. I hover in the upper corner of the room and look down at my body, then zoom in slowly until all my attention is on the side of my head. I concentrate and move forward and find myself in the tunnel that the bullet made. I have to go all the way across and make a u-turn where the slug bounced off the inside of my skull and backtracked. The walls of the tunnel are pink and glistening, with dried blood lining the bottom. The hole continues back and slightly downward and then—apparently another bounce off bone—makes a new start toward the center and upward before it stops. The lead slug is about two inches in from my skull and a quarter inch lower than the entry wound.

I re-enter my body and probe downward through tissue with the tweezers. A kaleidoscope of memories are triggered and probably erased forever as the steel slides through brain matter and meets lead. I grasp the slug and pull. The resistance is slight, like spooning jello, and, with a slight wet sound, out comes the prize, a .22 caliber bullet. Not much of a prize, but then I don't even like metal fillings in my teeth.

I see my face as it was when I was a child, unlined and unblemished, weeping silently. I put my hand to my cheek and feel tears tracking through the caked dust. The voice that has been instructing me changes—like in a dream when a car becomes a bicycle—into a book with the words moving across the page, telling me about threads: my life, and Ratboy's, and Jason Hamel's, Tanya's, Allison's, all interwoven at this point in a tapestry whose greater image I cannot discern. One of the threads separates out and becomes an image on a page in the book. It looks like a brown smear of feces, Ratboy's stain on my psyche. It shifts and the edges undulate and change like a Mandelbrot pattern. Brilliant colors and shapes emerge at the center and ripple out concentrically, mandala-like, and melt into the edges of the page. Each iteration is brighter and lighter than the one before it until, in the brilliant white of the paper, I am left not with the blot of Ratboy but the innocence of Jason Junior.

The book changes again, this time to a woman's voice, an angel I could embrace forever, telling me that healing is my birthright, that the healed state is my natural inheritance, that atonement is the only prerequisite to claiming it. I am presented with a choice and I assent.

I leave the body again and slip back into the hole. As I follow the bullet's original path, information wells up from an unknown source. Progenitors, directed tissue migration, mTOR pathways, PTEN inhibitors, growth factors, cytokines, all terms I've never heard of nor read about and yet now I know them as key terms in a set of instructions. I'm about to embark on a cellular repair project.

¤ ¤ ¤

I'm back in the body. I stand up and examine myself in the mirror. My nose is still too big, one eyelid still droops a bit, but the hole is repaired. And the one in my chest, as well as the shattered cheek and the back of my skull. There's a bald spot I can fix later, but the baseball cap is history.

Chapter 26

Mindy's voice comes from the doorway. "Dad, please, they're coming back!"

I get up and join her. A long cloud of dust trails a white pickup truck about a half a mile away to the south. My vision is crystal clear; there are more shades of green and brown than I ever dreamed of. The sky is a glazed-ceramic cerulean. The valley is almost in deep shadow so it must be late afternoon.

Herbie's binoculars show me a Ford F-150 with a roll bar and a man standing in the rear bed. The muffler must be gone because the engine's clattering roar fills the valley. Two men are in the cab. As they get closer I can see that they all have shaved heads with red marks—devils, I presume. The man standing in the rear is built like a stacked washer-drier set and is holding the roll bar with one hand and a shotgun in the other.

Mindy says, "These guys are really bad. We've got to get out of here."

I ask her if she's ready to run and she nods. We're hidden from view. I glance around the door jam and wait. The Ford is about fifty yards away and I put two holes in the windshield. The driver stomps on the brakes, fishtails the truck into a hard right and roars over the flat desert toward the east. The gunner in back fires in our direction as they speed away.

I grab Mindy's hand and we run toward Ratboy's van. The Ford has turned around and stopped, its idling engine booming. When we reach the van I tell Mindy to keep running up the road until she sees the Saturn.

The luck I need now is that the van will start. I pull out Ratboy's set of keys and find one that says Chevy on the black plastic end. I pull it off the keyring and put it in the ignition and turn it. The starter whines but the engine doesn't catch. The Ford starts rolling toward me.

I pull the remote-control device and the cell phones from the backpack and throw the pack in the rear of the van. I twist the key and the engine catches. The Ford closes half the distance as I back the van so that it's blocking the road. Boulders and shrubs extend outward on both sides so the van is impassable.

Gunshots erupt from the truck. The shotgun booms over the clatter of the engine. I exit the passenger side of the van and run up the hill after Mindy. The Ford stops at the van and the driver and the guy with the shotgun go to its driver and passenger doors. I can't see the third man. At forty yards I turn around and fire the .45's last two bullets, then I throw it away.

I catch up with Mindy at the gate and look back. The two Mexicans are back in the truck and are using it to push the van out of the way. Mindy's hand is on my shoulder; she's trembling. She says, "Dad, what are we going to do?"

I say, "Bad guys, right?"

Tears in her eyes, she nods.

I say, "Well, check this out," and I hit the red button on the remote.

A double explosion, first the C-4, then the van's gas tank, dwarfs the sound of the straining Ford. The smoke clears and we can see the charred hull of the van lying on its side about twenty feet from where it blew up. The Ford is butting heads with an immovable boulder, its engine screaming at redline. A huge, blackened corpse lies a distance back from where the Ford had been before the explosion.

We walk past the gate to the Saturn in silence.

Chapter 27

When Mindy was six, and all was still well in my world, we had a long-established ritual of splashing around in the community pool at the condo complex where we lived, and then soaking in the hot tub. One day, lounging with me in the jacuzzi, Mindy asked me, "Daddy, how did everything get here?"

I asked her what she meant by "everything" and she made a sweeping gesture to include the sky, the buildings, the trees, and said, "Everything there is."

So I told her there are two stories to explain it all. One is in the Bible, and it says that God created everything in six days. The other story is the one that science tells us, and it says that the universe popped into existence and kept getting bigger and that stuff formed over a really long time until it all turned into what we see today.

Mindy popped her head under the water and held her breath. When she emerged, she opened her eyes and said, "Well, which one do you believe?"

I said, "I'm inclined to go with science."

She asked, "How come?"

And I said, "Because I don't think God worked that fast."

A week later we were back in the hot tub and out of the blue Mindy asked me, "Daddy, what's the fastest thing in the world?"

"The speed of light, sweetie."

"And how fast does it go?"

"A hundred and eighty-six thousand miles per second."

"How fast is that?"

"It could go all the way around the world eight times between this . . ." I clapped my hands, "and this . . ." I clapped my hands again.

Mindy pondered this for a moment and said, "Dad?"

"Yeah?"

"If light can go around the world eight times that fast, why don't you think God could make everything in six days?"

I didn't have an answer for her.

¤ ¤ ¤

Now Mindy's asking me a question. "Dad? What do you think happens to them?"

I don't know what to tell her. That their threads have been snipped short in the weave? I know I'm not going to tell her my experience, partly because I don't know what it means, and partly because it's too much to lay on a fifteen-year-old who's just been through what Mindy's been through. I shake my head and tell her, "All I know is that now they can't hurt you."

We drive in silence. I want to get on the main road and put some miles behind us before the police come to investigate their second homicide by explosion for the day. At the creek bed, I stop the car and get out and fling DeShaun's gun far into a thicket of scrub brush.

¤ ¤ ¤

A sign says we're fifty-five kilometers from Ensenada, so we're a few miles north of where I left my car. The Z was predictably absent from the roadside, but that's all right.

153

I'm Paul Cleary, with my nice brilliant-blue Saturn. Which reminds me to ask Mindy, "You don't by any chance have any ID, do you?"

"Jesus, Dad, after all that just happened, you care about ID?"

"I care about ID because I want to get both of us across the border. I've had enough of Mexico, haven't you?"

Mindy's got her feet tucked up on the seat and her hands clasped to her knees. She says, "Hell yeah, but I could use a good meal pretty soon. And no, I don't have any ID, is that a problem?"

"Yeah, but I'll figure it out." An idea is forming in my head. It's awkward, but not nearly as much as having trouble at the border and going under closer scrutiny than the average returning Anglo tourist. I'm guessing that Paul Cleary is reported dead or missing somewhere. I still have my own driver's license, but the new law requires a passport to get back into the States.

"The house is gone, isn't it?"

"Gone."

"Jason told me that they had you tied to a chair in a basement somewhere and were going to kill you if I didn't come with him." She says this apologetically, as if I expected an explanation.

"Sweetie, there's nothing you could have done differently. I'm proud of you for getting through it, and that's all."

"Jason was pretty crazy. He didn't touch me, though. He, like, got obsessed with me. He said he was going to marry me when his dad got to Mexico. Then we got there and those creepy guys were living there. They started shooting at us so Jason took us to the cave. His dad was some kind of minister or something."

"I know."

"How did you know? And how come you dropped me off at the house and just disappeared? I mean, what's up with that? And, hey, when I woke up just before those guys in the truck came, you were staring in the mirror and for ten minutes I couldn't get you to break out of whatever trance you were in." Now she's getting agitated, which is good—she needs to make it all make sense. Trouble is, I don't know if I can help her there.

We're approaching Ensenada. I tell her, "Let's find a place to eat, and then I'll tell you what I can." In my new condition, I find the idea of eating to be appealing. The body seems to be operating on auto pilot, hungry, hot and sweating, alive. I turn on the air conditioning.

¤ ¤ ¤

Ensenada is a port town sixty miles south of the border. Cruise ships dock there and unload armies of tourists; rich attorneys from LA drive down in their Lexus SUVs for sport-fishing tournaments; surfers and college students and cheap honeymooners descend on the city for twenty-five cent beer and bargain hotels. On a hot August Saturday night, the place is crawling with *Norte Americanos* and the Mexicans who want their money; hawkers hawking weird tourist crap, barkers at the topless joints, pathetic looking six-year-olds selling Chicklets, drug hustlers, hookers, time-share salesmen, and cabbies handing out business cards for cheap dentistry and cosmetic surgery.

We keep passing restaurants that look like they are hosting frat parties, cross-streets too clogged to turn onto, and the occasional dark alley with plywood signs saying things like, "Steak & Lobstar $10." Now we're at San Miguel, the last stop, with its surf camp and tiny restaurant/bar and a crowd of people waiting outside to be seated.

I look at Mindy and say, "Another hour to Rosarito Beach. It might mellow out by then, what do you think?"

She lowers the back of her seat, stretches out, closes her eyes, and says, "I'm cool."

¤ ¤ ¤

I spend an hour driving in the dark while Mindy sleeps. The road narrows and climbs; it twists and turns to a point nearly a thousand feet above the ocean and then gradually descends all the way to Rosarito Beach. I wonder what to tell Mindy, how to explain the unexplainable, what to leave out and how to string the rest together so it still rings true. I'm having trouble with the ringing-true part.

Just before Rosarito is an odd little enclave of about thirty restaurants and the same number of tourist shops, plus a handful of liquor stores. The restaurants all serve the same thing: lobster. The tourist shops sell wood carvings of dolphins, mass manufactured in China, bobbling bugs in walnut shells, glass sea horses, bongo drums and maracas, and unplayable guitars and ukuleles. I enter through the twin arches and find a place to park in a mud lot at the end of the main drag. Reaching out to Mindy, I massage her shoulder gently with my fingers and say, "Hey, time to eat."

We pick a restaurant at random because it doesn't matter. This one is up a narrow flight of stairs and probably has a great view in the daytime but now just looks out on darkness. We sit next to the giant window separating us from the darkness; the crowd has already eaten, chips and salsa arrive immediately, I am ravenous. We order our dinners with our mouths stuffed with chips. I can taste the salt and feel the heat of the chilies; could it be that I am really restored?

The waiter returns for our order. He looks us over and says, "Been camping long?"

I tell him that we have been exploring caves at a gold mine and that the amenities were minimal. He blinks and concentrates on his order pad. I ask him what he suggests and he says, "The langosta is very excellent, señor." The last thing I ate was jail food, so nearly anything would be very excellent. Mindy and I both point to the same thing on the menu and ask for iced tea as well.

When we've crunched through all the chips, Mindy looks up and says, "Well?"

I say, "Let's swap stories, one thing at a time, okay?"

"Fine, you first." We should have stopped for a comb at a liquor store; Mindy's hair is crazed and streaked with dirt, her face sunburned and thinner than usual.

"Okay. The thing about me and the mirror, back at the mine?"

"Yeah?"

"I can't explain it. Sorry. It's too weird."

"Oh, so now it's my turn?"

I shrug.

"Fine. Jason kept giving me some kind of drug to keep me quiet. It was a crappy high and then I'd fall asleep."

I tell her how I left her at the house and went to Jimmy's and that he had been shot and his place ransacked.

She says, "Isn't he, like, your drug connection?" Allison leaves no stone unturned.

"He was, but I'm done with all that."

"For real?"

"For real."

"So then what happened?"

"I spent the next thirty hours in the LA County jail. It wasn't fun. When I got out, I tried calling you. Then I came home and it was gone. My neighbor Cal told me he had seen you leaving with two guys."

"So what did they want?" Mindy asks as the waiter comes with our food. We dive into it and I look for a short answer.

"They were part of a case I was working on. Stolen money. Jason's father was involved, but he's dead now."

Mindy looks surprised. "Jason kept telling me his father was on his way."

"Jason's friend shot at me and missed. He hit Jason's father instead."

"Luke did that?" Mindy's sitting there, open-mouthed, looking at me with an expression like I'm bull-shitting her or something.

"If that's his name, yeah. Jason's giant friend."

"Luke was really sweet. He took care of me and calmed Jason down every time he started to get crazy. What happened to them, anyway?"

I crack the shell of my lobster and pull the meat out. Mindy stares at me and says, "Dad?"

"We had a disagreement about your being in Mexico unconscious in a cave."

"Yeah? Go on."

"It wasn't settled with words."

We finish our meals in silence.

¤ ¤ ¤

We tramp through mud back to the Saturn. An August squall has hit the coast, and warm, fat drops of rain fall on us and make the air smell good. The backpack is in the rear seat. Of the three cell phones, only Jason Hamel's has any juice left, plus bars so I can make a call. I fish in my pocket and pull out the card that my former neighbor gave me for Dave Putnam, the writing detective, and punch in the number.

"Yes." Not a question, and not very friendly.

"Dave, Charlie Miner."

"Well, Charlie Miner! I was just thinking, I love it when dead people call me."

I have no idea what to say to that. Maybe I should have texted him instead.

"I would really like to hear the story of why you're using a homicide victim's cell phone."

Okay, that's easier to explain. In fact, I have a plan for that.

"Dave, I'll do you one better and then some, but I need a favor."

"I'm all ears." Actually, he's a really big guy with unusually small ears, but now's not the time to crack wise.

"Here's what I've got for you. I can help you close, count 'em, one, two, three murder cases. And I can give you a scam that maybe even you haven't seen yet. You can write a whole book on the story I give you, but I don't know how it ends yet."

"Which three murders are you talking about?"

"I'll give it all up tomorrow, after you help me out."

"How about I just pick you up on suspicion, since you're the guy with Jason Hamel's phone?"

"Good luck with that. I'm in Mexico. Work with me here, I'm in over my head."

"What do you want?"

"You know my house burned down—"

"Yeah," Dave interrupts. "While you were in Central Booking."

"I'm glad you know so much about me. Look, my daughter was in the house, and the creeps that torched it kidnapped her and brought her down here. Now I've got her but she's got no ID so I can't get her through Immigration."

"And you want me to drive down there and get her? What am I, your goddamned shuttle service?"

"Three murders and a scam, Dave." I remember Jimmy and say, "And an attempted murder."

A long silence, and then a sigh. "All right, Charlie. When and where?"

"Rosarito Beach Hotel, ten tomorrow."

We click off and I start the car.

¤ ¤ ¤

We're heading north again.

Mindy says, "So I get a ride home in a cop car? Sounds like a fun way to end my vacation." I'm not in the mood for snarky, but I let it go. We're quiet for a minute until she says, "Sorry Dad. I guess we've both been through some pretty weird shit."

"A whole new standard of weird."

"You're not sending me back to Mom's, are you?"

"Got any better ideas?"

"Not yet, but something good better come up. She smacked me hard last time and you know what?"

"Tell me."

"If there's a next time, I'm fighting back and it won't be pretty."

"I hear you. I'll see what I can come up with." There's a place in Venice we could probably camp out in, if we can get past DeShaun and his crew.

"You know, Jason didn't kidnap me on his own. He was supposed to take me somewhere in Century City, but the whole time we were at his apartment he just stared at me. He was really high on something. And then he says, 'Me and you, we're Adam and Eve.' Then he told Luke we were changing plans and going to Mexico. That's when he called his dad and asked him to marry us. He took pictures of us together with his cell phone and sent them to his dad."

"I know, I saw them."

"So then he got this call and afterwards he's all panicky and we got in his car and went to someplace in Santa Monica Canyon."

"This is yesterday afternoon?"

"Yeah. We go up this long driveway and your car was there. So Luke and Jason get out of the car and tell me to stay put. I saw Luke fire a gun into the big window and then heard another shot from inside the house, and then they both came running back to the car. Jason's shirt was all bloody. I was scared that you got shot."

"One of Luke's bullets killed Jason's dad. One of mine hit Jason in the shoulder."

"So then Jason's freaking out and talking all kinds of crazy stuff."

"Yeah, like what?"

"He would quote the Bible a lot, but I think he messed up the quotes. He called the cave in Mexico the eye of the needle. He'd say stuff like, 'Can the Ethiopian change his spots? I think not.' Then he talked about how he was just trying to fix everything for his dad, but that his Uncle Alan messed everything up."

"What did he mean by that?"

"I don't know, I think he was on speed. He talked so much I stopped listening. We made a quick stop at his place and swapped the Mustang for a van and drove to the mine."

"And when you got there?"

"As soon as we got past that gate someone started shooting at us. Luke shot back and I guess he got two of them. Another one drove away in that Ford truck. That's when we went to the cave."

We're pulling into the Rosarito Beach area. I park in front of one of the smaller hotels and we get out. Mindy says, "So whose car is this, anyway?"

Chapter 28

We walk up to the desk in the lobby and I ask for a room. The clerk is a middle-aged Mexican woman with hair pulled back so tight it's pulling at the corners of her eyes. She checks us out and then looks at me like I'm a dirtbag and it's probably not because we look like we've been camping. I hand over eighty bucks of Jason Hamel's money and we navigate a dank concrete hallway until we get to our room. Everything smells of Pine-Sol and the lighting is dim. There's a king-size bed, a TV on a stand, a few chairs, and a desk.

Mindy says, "I'm gonna take a bath and wash my clothes. Want me to do yours?" and steps into the bathroom. I strip to my shorts and hand her my clothes and lie down. I pull the bedcover over myself to leave the actual sheets and blanket to Mindy. The sound of water running becomes a consuming roar and then fades.

¤ ¤ ¤

I'm sitting in Father Tomas's church with a bare light bulb swaying slightly just above my head. Everything is in shades of grey, going pitch dark outside the small perimeter of the bulb's glow. A man walks up to my pew but I can't see his face. A sense of dread prevents me from looking at him. I feel heat radiating from him, as if he were on fire. He says, "Who are you trying to kid? You can't fix dead."

I try to respond; my mouth moves but only muted gibberish comes out.

The man says, "You know where the money is."

I shake my head. The floor is strewn with gold: gold coins, gold teeth, rings, little bars stamped "SUISSE, 10 OUNCES FINE GOLD, 99.9." There's a slender gold vase with a single red rose in it. I shake my head harder; I put my whole body into it, an emphatic denial; the pieces of gold rattle as the floor starts undulating.

"Dad, wake up! It's okay, just wake up." Mindy is pushing my shoulder, shoving me, the bed is moving, and the dread subsides as I look at her, bewildered and relieved.

¤ ¤ ¤

My clothes are almost dry. Good enough for breakfast, anyway. Lobster omelet, of course, is the house special. We pass and order huevos rancheros; last day of vacation, eat like a local.

It's ten sharp and the morning is hot and moist already. Dave Putnam pulls up in an unmarked charcoal Dodge Charger. He rolls down his window and says, "Taxi?"

I already prepped Mindy on what to say: Some freak kidnapped her and took her to Mexico and her dad came down and got her back. Period. "My dad'll fill you in. Hey, I hear you write books. You must have all kinds of interesting stories." Dave's a smart guy and a pro at interrogation, but if she can hold out until we get across the border, I'll handle him from there.

I introduce Mindy to Dave; they shake hands through his window. Dave looks at me skeptically and says, "So what's the plan?"

I want to laugh and tell him: *Plan? What plan? There are only threads that are people following their own motives, creating a picture they can't comprehend. How can we even dream of a plan?* Instead, I say, "Meet me at the Denny's on the right just across the border. After that, we'll meet up in LA later today and I'll lay it all out for you."

He shakes his head and reaches across to open the Dodge's passenger door. Mindy gives me a peck on the cheek and gets in the car.

It is eighteen miles to the US. I follow Dave's car into Tijuana through the maze of twists and turns that lead to the border. A sign says *LINEA SENTRI* and the traffic gets worse. We're bumper to bumper, inching forward past giant billboards advertising beer and booze and politicians. We pass a structure that looks like a mescaline-induced cubist totem pole. A one-legged vendor thrusts a churro at my window. I shake my head and he hobbles on to feed the cars behind me. Women dressed as nurses hold out cans for donations; old men offer plaster Tweety Birds, sunglasses, cactuses in pots, monkey puppets on strings attached to the ends of sticks, and a plaster Mary with a halo of concentric shiny wire rings.

Concrete dividers force the traffic into separate lanes. A VW bus with surfboards on top is stalled in the lane next to me. The driver of the truck behind him leans on his horn. His bumper sticker says IF YOU CAN'T FEED 'EM, DON'T BREED 'EM. I follow Dave past them and we're within sight of the customs stations.

I pull out my wallet and the passport Herbie made for me. They look pretty shabby after getting soaked in Ratboy's sacred stream. I pull out my real driver's license and hide it in my sock. If I had a plan, I would have told Dave we needed a Plan B in case Paul Cleary didn't make it across the border.

Dave shows his wallet; the sun flashes off his gold shield and the border guard waves him through. I pull up and say, "Good morning," and hand him my license and passport.

"Got anything to declare?"

"Nope."

"Stay right there." He goes into a little booth and confers with a man in a white shirt and tie. The man shakes his head. The border guard comes back and holds up my passport.

"This looks pretty bad."

"Got wet. What can I say?"

He hands it back to me. "You'll probably want to replace it. Especially if you're planning on going overseas."

"You bet."

"New one's a hundred and forty bucks. Sorry about that." And he waves me through.

¤ ¤ ¤

Dave gets out of his car and looks at his watch. "Two hours. Not bad."

"I owe you. You won't be disappointed."

"So what's next?"

"It's noon. Two hours at least to get to LA, and I've got stops to make. I'll try for five."

"Where?"

"Santa Monica somewhere. We can sort that out by phone later. You okay with that?"

"I'm not okay with this whole thing, but hey . . ." He gives a dismissive wave, "Whatever. If I don't hear from you, I'm gonna hunt you down."

"Got it."

"And you're gonna tell me what happened in Mexico."

Mindy's out of the car now. She looks at me and shrugs. Dave says, "Some freak kidnapped her and took her to Mexico and you went down and got her back. Cute."

Mindy puts out her hand and says, "Bye. And thanks for the cool stories."

Dave glares at me and gets back in the Charger.

¤ ¤ ¤

We drive in silence. It's okay. I'm whole, the world is alive, the freeway and landscape and sky are sparkling with color. Mindy is safe, and I have, if not a plan, at least a few ideas about where to go. We stop for coffee in Carlsbad and get back on the 5.

Mindy bites into a scone and says, "He comes on like he's mean, but he's really a nice guy."

"I know. We go back a ways."

"He told me some hysterical stories about people he's busted. Criminals are really dumb."

"Yep. Most of them." I wonder about that, though, because somebody's got eight mil of Tanya's husband's money, and right now they're looking pretty clever.

Going through Torrance, I see a Wal-Mart right by an off-ramp. There are a few things we should get, so we pull off the freeway and into the parking lot.

Mindy pushes a cart while I grab what we need: jeans and tee shirts for both of us, cheap shoes and socks, underwear, deodorant, toothbrushes, and a car charger for all three phones. I pay with just about the last of Jason's money.

Mindy says, "Okay, we're stylin' now."

I turn onto the Marina Freeway and we cruise toward the beach. My phone is the first to charge.

"This is for emergency only. Please don't call your friends and chat. You've got one day's charge and I want to be able to reach you on the first ring."

"What do you mean, reach me? Where are you taking me and where are you going?"

"I'm taking you to Ratboy's."

"Whose?"

"Jason Junior's. I think of him as Ratboy. Like in the movie."

"Guess I missed that one, Dad. What am I supposed to do there?"

"Lie low until I come back. Remember what you told me, Jason kidnapped you on someone else's instruction?"

"Yeah..."

"Well, that someone is still out there."

"Some guy kept calling him while we were driving to Mexico. Jason told him stuff like, 'No, the plan's changed,' and, 'No, not gonna do that.'"

"Do you know who it was?"

"Yeah, because every time it would end up with Jason hanging up all flipped out and screaming about his fucking Uncle Alan."

"Did fucking Uncle Alan know you were going to Mexico?"

"Definitely. And he knew there was a mine down there." A tumbler clicks into place in my brain and another memory is unlocked: Tanya, her lizard-skin cowboy boots up on my desk, telling me that she had been referred to me by Alan Hunter.

A right on Lincoln Boulevard takes us north into Venice. Ratboy's might be safe; if Uncle Alan thinks Ratboy is still in Mexico and has a reason to check the apartment, he's probably already been there. And why would he go there in the first place?

I cruise by the Flora, checking for warning signs, cops, Crips, vehicles that don't look right. It's two in the afternoon and hot, and the street is quiet. A right at the corner and another into an alley take me to the back of the apartment building where the parking stalls are. A silver Mustang is parked next to an empty spot; both spots have the number "11" stenciled on them. I pull into the empty space and turn off the ignition. I look at Mindy and say, "Well, last chance. Got any better ideas?"

"Nope. Anyway, this makes sense. He took your home from us, so we should get his for a while."

The back stairs go right up to number 11. No one seems to be watching, or no one cares. Ratboy's key lets us in. It's dreary and fairly disgusting, but it's home for now. We head to Ratboy's room. Its fastidious neatness and the sun coming in through the lightly curtained window convey the feel of a well-behaved teenager's room, Ratboy's way of putting a gloss on his pathology.

Chapter 29

The Mustang purrs, quiet but powerful. I look out the passenger window toward the parked Saturn. A bullet went out that window and tunneled through my brain. Ratboy sat in the seat next to me and fired the bullet. I'm in the driver's seat now, still without a plan, but having no plan has brought me to some interesting places so far.

I had a fascinating conversation before I left the apartment. After programming Jason Hamel's cell number into my phone for Mindy, I found Alan Hunter's number in his directory. I dialed it and got a response on the first ring.

"Who is this?" It wasn't a question, but a demand.

"Charlie Miner. Got time for a chat?"

"You're a very clever fellow for a washed-up junky PI."

"Right. Is that why you recommended me to Tanya?"

"She needed an expendable middleman who wouldn't get too nosy. My bad."

"Are you at your office?"

"Yes. We should have a face-to-face. Where are you?"

I told him I was in the Valley and listened while he gave me his office address.

Lincoln to the 10 to the 405 to Santa Monica Boulevard takes me to his law firm's Century City penthouse. I park the Mustang and ride up the elevator in my new Wal-

Mart jeans and tee shirt. I'm still contemplating the word "expendable" when a secretary ushers me into Hunter's office.

Alan Hunter remains seated but gestures toward a chair facing his desk, which is a rich, deep brown with a hint of red, polished to a shine. He probably has matching tasseled loafers. The desk is a mile wide and has nothing on it but Hunter's elbows. His fingers are steepled, his fingertips resting against his lips. He doesn't seem interested in shaking my hand.

I decide to kick it off. "Thanks for the referral, but so far it's been a clusterfuck."

Hunter looks like a movie star in the traditional mold: tanned, aristocratic, slightly graying at the temples, and poised. Only his eyes give him away as a street fighter, a predator's patient calculating of odds and possibilities hidden in his unblinking gaze.

He decides to smile and unleashes a dazzling display of perfect teeth and human warmth as he puts his hands on the desk and says, "I was rude to you on the phone, Mr. Miner. I believe we can help each other, and I apologize for my behavior."

I'm not buying it, but I pretend to. "No problem. Call me Charlie. How can I help you?" I know he's not giving up anything that won't help him, and he'll deliver that in his own time, but I'm curious what he thinks I can do for him.

"Well, I'm missing four million dollars of my own money in this clusterfuck, as you call it. I think you might be able to help me find it." A scene from a dream flits through my mind: A man I can't look at says, *You know where my money is.*

"Maybe it's where my house is."

Hunter lifts his eyebrows. "You think I'm responsible for that?"

"Somebody set me up, shot at me, set my house on fire, and kidnapped my daughter. I'm just following my instincts."

He pounces. "Do you know where they took your daughter?"

"Who's 'they'?"

"He, she, how should I know? Is your daughter safe?"

"How should I know?" It's tempting to smirk, but the man behind the squeaky-clean desk is a no-bullshit guy and I'm not ready to test his limit.

He tilts his head and looks at me like he's considering a new tack, then nods. "I'll tell you what. I'm a father myself and I don't like what's happening here. You deserve to know what has happened to you, and I can fill you in on a rough outline of it."

"Okay. I'm listening."

"First, I want to know one thing."

"What's that?"

"Why do you have Jason Hamel's phone?"

It might have been sloppy of me to call him from Jason's cell. On the other hand, what does it matter?

"I took it from him after he got shot."

"You mean you didn't shoot him?

"Now why would I do that? No, I didn't shoot him. The same guys that shot at me before tried again but hit him instead."

"And who might they be?" The man plays dumb with considerable confidence.

"A skinny kid with a face like a rat and his linebacker sidekick."

Alan Hunter shakes his head slowly, as if something he had long expected finally came about, some irrevocable act that finally reveals itself as having always been inevitable. He almost looks sad.

"Do you know where they went after this happened?"

"I have no idea. But my neighbor saw them leaving my house with my daughter just before it burned down." I can play dumb with confidence too.

We stare at each other across the giant desk. He says he's got four million bucks on the line, and for some reason he thinks I'm the key to retrieving it. He sighs and shrugs and says, "I'm the kid's godfather. He calls me Uncle Alan. Jason Hamel and Mickey Peterson—that's Tanya's husband—and I went to college together. He calls Mickey Uncle Mick. We've known him ever since Jason and Julia adopted him over twenty years ago."

I'd like to correct him to the past tense on Ratboy, but why give my hand away? I just say, "Okay," and wait for him to go on.

"He's always been a problem, developmentally challenged, ADHD, impulsive behavior, drugs. But he's not the real problem here."

"Somebody set him in motion."

"Exactly. But he's a loose cannon, there's no controlling him, and he's cunning but not very bright."

"What do you want to tell me?"

Hunter stares at me again, unblinking as a snake, taking his time, unconcerned with the weirdness he's generating. A minute goes by. I check my watch and tell him, "Well, it's been fascinating, but..." and I start to get up.

He interrupts with his palm thrust out at me, ordering me to stop. He says, "Let me be frank. You're bumbling through a minefield without a map of the terrain. You've been used and useless and your life is in danger. So is your daughter's. What you don't realize is that I'm on your side."

"How's that, Alan?"

"Who do you think got you out of jail?"

"I haven't given it much thought. It's been a busy few days."

"And aren't you curious why there were no charges? You weren't given a date for a court appearance. Do you think that all happened by magic?"

I remember thinking it was strange that Tanya knew just when to show up when I got processed out of County, but it didn't seem critical at the time and then I just forgot about it.

Alan Hunter reaches into his jacket pocket and pulls out a checkbook. He opens it, looks up at me, and says, "Three thousand, right?"

"That was before my house burned down, my car got stolen, and my daughter got kidnapped." And a bullet bored through my brain.

"This is about keeping agreements. Tanya's agreement was for three thousand dollars." He writes the figure on the check and signs it with a flourish. He rolls his chair slightly back and opens the top drawer of his desk and pulls out a gun, puts it on the desk with his hand over it, and says, "Let me tell you a story."

Chapter 30

The gun is a Smith and Wesson .38 Special with a space-age grip and an alloy body. It's lying there, pointing at me, next to the check. Hunter keeps his hand resting lightly on it.

"Mickey Peterson is a compulsive gambler, an alcoholic, and a very desperate man. When he found out that there was a report signed by our geologist stating that the project in Mexico was worthless, he panicked. He wanted to suppress it until he could pull his cash out, but first he had to find it."

"And Tanya beat him to it."

"Exactly. She stole it from me."

"Let me guess—while you were sleeping, with a little assistance from Rohypnol."

"Last thing I remember was her whispering, 'Lights out, baby.' Tanya's very resourceful. She wanted the money because it was undeclared cash and she was going to leave the country with it. So she tried to leverage the report against Jason Hamel because he had collected the funds for the corporation. When Mickey found out that she was trying to negotiate with Jason, he sent Jason Junior out to kill the transaction and anyone facilitating it."

"Why would the kid do that for him?"

"Because good old Uncle Mick had always been the nice guy, the enabler, the guy who said, 'Oh, he's just a kid, lighten up.' He taught the kid how to drink and how to roll a joint when he was twelve. And he taught him how to shoot a gun."

"But the kid showed up at the restaurant to pick up the briefcase for his father."

"That's what the father thought too, but the kid was playing him. That's why Hamel stopped the transaction; I figured out what was happening and told him just in time. Of course, Jason wanted to suppress the report for his own reasons."

"He told me he was convinced it was a mistake, and that the mine had huge potential. He smelled a rat somewhere."

"You talked to him?"

"Yes, we had a conversation while I watched him die."

"Then you probably know he was a zealot who believed that God was going to deliver him a jackpot so he could fund his own ministry."

"He said something along those lines. Could you point the gun away from me now? It's distracting me from the conversation."

Hunter smiles down at the gun and turns it slightly so it won't blow a hole in me if his finger twitches.

"When Jason Junior failed to retrieve the papers, Mickey went crazy and ordered the kidnapping. Burning your house was the kid's idea, in case the report was somewhere in it."

"So you have no idea where my daughter is."

"I believe my godson may have taken her to Mexico, to the mine."

"Is that part of Mickey's plan?"

"No, that's part of Junior's plan. He got high and developed a psychotic infatuation with your daughter. He thinks they're eloping. I tried to talk him into bringing her here but he yelled at me and hung up."

"What good would the report do Mickey now that Jason's dead and the money's gone?" The pieces fit weirdly and the black hole at the end of the gun seems to have drifted back in my direction.

"There's a doctored report that Jason Hamel manufactured. He forged a document saying that the mine hosts a huge deposit. Mickey still wants to take the company public through the Vancouver Exchange; then he can run up the share price with the forged report and sell his director's shares and recoup some money."

"So if I just give him the damned reports he'll back off?" They're in my back pocket, but they're barely readable now.

Hunter glances at the gun. "You have them with you?"

"I have access to them." I glance at the black hole.

"I'm afraid it's more complicated than that."

"Really. How's that?"

"He thinks you killed Hamel and stole the money. He says if you don't give it to him by tonight, he's going to kill your ex-wife."

I burst out laughing. "Boy, he's pretty clueless then. You mean he'd do it for free?"

"It may amuse you, but I doubt if it would amuse your daughter." He looks at his watch and says, "It's half past three. You'll probably find him at the Normandie Casino. Here..." He hands me the check and then slides the gun toward me. "You might need this."

Chapter 31

I jam the Mustang out from the underground parking into daylight, my knuckles white from the death grip I have on the steering wheel, a metallic taste in the back of my throat, and a tic in my jaw. The insanity of the past five days is catching up to me, engulfing me; I feel a fine-edged rage vibrating like an electric guitar string in my brain.

Allison is family. She's Mindy's mother and I'm tired of being a pinball in someone's arcade game. I remember the voice speaking through the static: "Retribution is allowed." And I'm ready to deliver. Part of me dispassionately watches my rage as it consumes me.

¤ ¤ ¤

The Normandie is the only original Southern California card club still in existence. When the state made gambling illegal back in the 1880s, it exempted poker because the legislators loved the game. In 1936, The Normandie Casino was opened in Gardena. At one point it generated most of the operating funds for the city. Now there are gambling joints all over, but the Normandie has its own clientele and continues to take money from people while they think they're having fun.

If you've been to one casino, you've been to them all. Even the most upscale ones have a seedy edge, like a Playboy club with yesterday's bunnies. The Normandie is popular with the Asian crowd and has games like PaiGow and Pan 9. The chatter at the tables has a musical quality you won't find at the Hustler or Hawaiian Gardens. I walk past the baccarat tables, blackjack, three-card poker, and Omaha high-low split, until I get to the main event: Texas hold 'em.

Mickey Peterson is as hard to miss as Madonna at an AME Church service. He's as Irish as Old Bushmills, red face, red hair, and built like a bulldog. Right now he's sweating like a fat man in a sauna, a small pile of chips and a drink on the table in front of him. I watch him down the drink and push out another chip. A Vietnamese man with an unlit cigarette dangling from his lower lip takes the pot and Peterson wipes his forehead with the sleeve of his coat.

I wave for a waitress and order a double of whatever he's drinking with a tall water back, delivered to Mickey. For twenty bucks, it better be Armagnac, but I'm not complaining. I back up a few tables and watch him deplete his pile of chips, buy more, and drink the double.

It takes about fifteen minutes before he's done and dismounts ponderously from his seat. I follow him across the room toward the restaurant. He lurches past daytime diners and broke liquid-lunchers nursing cups of coffee and navigates past a pay phone into the men's room. I follow him in and watch him unzip at the urinal.

I pull the gun out of a recyclable market bag I borrowed from Alan Hunter's receptionist that says "Keep it Green." When I pull it back, the hammer makes a distinctive click that startles Mickey Peterson out of his stupor. He turns and looks at me and backs up. Urine sprays on the floor at my feet in a diminishing arc and finally splashes his shoes.

Most alcoholics manage to achieve a permanent condition of half-in-the-bag, but Mickey's all the way in it; the old boy is boiled as an owl, snockered, three sheets to the wind, and long gone. He looks down at his prick and gives it a quick tug before tucking it into his pants. He leaves his fly open and tries to focus on me. His mouth hangs open and his nose is wrinkled in concentration.

"Who the fuck are you?" It's a garbled snarl, and the wire in my brain sings a higher, shriller note. I push him backward into the handicapped stall and lock the door behind me. He stumbles back and lands with his ass wedged between the toilet and the wall, his feet up on the seat and his arm propped up by the toilet paper dispenser. I move in, my hand steady, the wire thrumming. I have nothing to say that a bullet won't say better.

Peterson's eyes focus. He blinks his eyes and blurts, "You fucked my wife, didn't you, you miserable prick." He struggles to get up. I move toward him, the muzzle touches his forehead; he glares at me with a rage of his own. I squeeze the trigger; it has a mile-long pull, every millimeter takes a lifetime and the destination is eternity delivered from a black hole. The roaring in my head starts; the voice bleeds through and I remember its warning, killing of innocents, and I realize that I can't shoot this pathetic fool, that I've been set up, and that the snake-eyed predator in his Century City penthouse office is still a step ahead of me.

Chapter 32

I helped Mickey Peterson up into a sitting position on the toilet and left him sobbing in the stall. A Chinese in a Hawaiian shirt washed his hands and looked at me suspiciously in the mirror as I left.

I'm heading north out of Gardena in the Mustang. Dave calls: "You ready to get together?"

"Soon."

"Where are you?"

"I'm running around town like a rat in a maze. Cheese everywhere, and it all stinks."

"Let me help you."

"I'll call soon. Count on it." I thumb the phone off. It rings again.

"Dad?"

"Mindy, hey, are you all right?"

"Yeah, I'm fine. I'm just cleaning the place up. The kitchen was really gross."

"I know. Has anyone called my phone?"

"Mom called, and someone named Tanya. I didn't answer, so maybe they left messages. Are you coming back soon?"

I don't know what I'm doing. There is no indicated next step. I'd like to go back to Century City and show Alan Hunter a close-up of a bullet, but rats don't chase cats without a plan.

"Yeah, soon. Still got some errands to do." Like what, grocery shopping? I've got no ID, so the check is useless. I'm out of cash, low on gas, and bankrupt in the idea department.

"Dad?"

"What, sweetheart?"

"I just remembered something Jason told Luke while we were driving in Mexico."

"What's that?"

"He said his father told him that if anything bad happened to him—to his dad—that he should remember the rose garden."

This time different memories assemble themselves as if I'm picking up a perfect hand of poker, one card at a time.

Jason Hamel, bleeding to death in front of me. I ask him where the money is and he says, "It's all in the ground..."

Tanya telling me that's geo-speak for gold that hasn't been dug up yet.

My dream about a church floor strewn with gold and a vase with a rose in it.

Jason Hamel's website, telling the world that "the dollar bears the Mark of The Beast."

Hamel's jungle of a yard, and the one patch of carefully tended roses.

I know where the money is. And I know what it will look like.

"Dad, are you still there?"

"Sorry, I'm driving and hit a spot of traffic. I'll see you soon."

¤ ¤ ¤

It's half past six in the evening on a Sunday, and traffic is pretty light. The tunnel at the end of the Santa Monica Freeway spits me out onto the Pacific Coast Highway. The sun is heading toward the horizon and the ocean looks smooth as glass.

The Mustang crunches over the gravel in Jason Hamel's driveway. I'm banking on the place being deserted. There's still crime-scene tape at the door, but I'm not going inside.

I walk around the side of the house to the back and find the shovel I knew would be there. There's a path curving down through the bushes to a small gate and the street. A pair of gloves sits on a spool of wound-up garden hose. I put them on.

The roses were looking better the last time I was here. Two days in the summer heat and nobody to water them has left the petals drooping and curling at the edges. The shovel bites into the dirt, which is surprisingly soft, and slips under the root system. I move around the first plant and dig carefully. There are three plants in a row over about five feet of garden plot. I uproot each of them and set them against the house. A small mound of dirt piles up as I dig deeper. It's hot and I'm sweating as the sky darkens.

At about three feet down I hit something solid. I remove the dirt and find a rectangular piece of plywood. Underneath is a plastic tarp. I lift it up and see two rows of three SentrySafe H2300 fire-safe, waterproof chests. I lift one out and find another set of chests underneath, twelve in all.

On a hunch, I pull out Ratboy's keys. There's one small key that wouldn't fit a standard door lock. The chest opens and shows a fitted plastic foam inner lid. I pull it off and strike gold.

I don't know much about the stuff, but I know it's been on a roll for the last few years. There's a conspiracy theory that says that the United States has sold all its gold and replaced the bars at Fort Knox with fake ones filled with tungsten. When the world finds out the US has nothing but counterfeit gold, faith in the dollar will finally crumble and gold will become the new world currency.

What I do know is that, at fourteen hundred bucks an ounce, a four-hundred-ounce brick is worth over half a million dollars, and I'm staring at two of them nestled into cavities carved into the lower foam casing in the chest. I pry one out and examine it. There's an assay stamp, a date, and a serial number. It's only about seven inches long and weighs almost thirty pounds.

I set the bar back in the foam cavity and close the lid on the chest. Three more chests and I've got Mickey Peterson's investment sitting on the ground. Replacing the plastic tarp and the plywood, I shovel the dirt back into the hole, carefully replanting the rose bushes. I leave the shovel by the side of the house where I found it and carry the chests back to the Mustang.

I call Mindy and tell her I'm on my way, and then dial Dave's number.

"What?"

"Meet me at Chez Jay in forty-five minutes."

"Fine. This better be good."

Good enough for me.

Chapter 33

indy lets me in and makes a grand gesture toward the living room and kitchen. The place has been transformed, and the work seems to have been good for Mindy; she grins and does a little pirouette.

I hand her some takeout I stopped for on the way. She thanks me and digs in; with her mouth full of pad thai noodles she says, "Your friend Jimmy called. I answered, is that okay?"

"Yeah, that's good. What did he say?"

"He told me to tell you he's okay and he should be out tomorrow."

"Out of the hospital, or out of jail?"

"I don't know. Both, I guess. He said to call him at his mom's, and he left a number."

I tell Mindy to hold on a minute. There's a desk in Ratboy's room. I pull a sheet of paper from his printer and compose a note:

Jimmy,

Glad you're okay.

If you're reading this note, I'm gone.

Check the Mustang's trunk.

One for you. One for Cynthia Caffey—she's listed in West Hollywood under James Caffey. Two for Mindy—wash it, pay tax, put it in trust, and give her mom $100,000 to keep her copacetic.

Find BH stockbroker named Mickey Peterson and give him the enclosed papers.

Good luck,

CM

There's an envelope in the drawer; I put in the letter and the reports and write Jimmy's name on it.

Mindy has wolfed down the entire dinner. She's in a good mood.

"Can we go to a movie or do something normal like that?

"I'm sorry, but I've got two more errands." Her expression changes. "Then this should be over. Promise."

"I really want to get out of here. Just for a little while, please?"

"Look, one last thing. I've got to do it. If it all goes well, we can go anywhere. How about Mexico in style, like a cruise?"

She shakes her head.

"Hawaii, then. A week in Maui to clear our heads. We'll learn to surf together."

Now she brightens again and says, "Okay, Dad, but be careful."

"Right. Which brings me to one last thing." I hand her the envelope. "If anything happens to me, I want you to call Jimmy and give him this."

Mindy's chin goes up and her eyes are shiny. She accepts the envelope without a word, along with the keys to the Mustang. We hug for a full minute—I can't let go—a love as big as grief consumes me.

I walk out the door.

¤ ¤ ¤

I drive the Saturn up Lincoln to Ocean Park Boulevard and turn right on Nielson Way. Chez Jay stands alone between a motel parking lot and a fenced-in lot, half a block south of the Santa Monica Pier. It looks like a dive but serves some of the best food in Los Angeles. It has a history of movie stars and dope dealers, Old Hollywood and hangers-on, and an owner with a legendary secret weapon.

People are waiting but Dave has a booth in the back.

"Nice tee shirt."

My shirt is smeared with dirt from Jason Hamel's rose garden. I shrug and sit opposite him.

"I ordered for you. If your story's as good as you say, steak's on me. If it's garbage, you've got bigger problems than a dinner bill." He takes a pull from a big glass of iced amber liquid, Johnnie Walker Black if I remember correctly.

"You drinking on the job?"

"I'm not on the job."

I start from the beginning with Tanya showing up at my house, and he interrupts me already.

"Mickey Peterson's wife? Jesus, I've seen her picture. She's hot. What's in the briefcase?"

"Two reports about a gold investment. They contradict each other."

"Which one's real?"

"The one that says the investment is a bust." I go on to explain the stock scam and why everyone was scrambling for the geologist's reports.

"So the broad wants to blackmail this Hamel character for her husband's money so she can disappear with it."

"Right. And her husband wants the report so he can get his money out before the other investors tie everything up in court."

"So where's the money?"

"I'm going to take you to it."

Our meals arrive. We chew steak for a while. The place is buzzing around us, but we're in a bubble of our own: the smell of our food, the clink of ice in Dave's glass, the occasional glance as he looks up at me, the muted colors in the low light. What did Alan Hunter say—I'm bumbling through a minefield without a map of the terrain?

Dave puts down his knife and fork and says, "All right. Three homicides. Jason Hamel's one of them, right?"

"Three homicides and two more attempted. Yeah, Hamel's one."

"Walk me through it."

"Let me start with the first attempted. That would be on me, the night I tried to deliver the papers." I tell him about the interrupted handoff at the Cheesecake Factory and how I got shot at while riding my bike home. I leave out the part about getting high at Jimmy's and, of course, the matter of the bullet in my brain.

"So this guy you met at the restaurant waits for you and shoots at you. What happened?"

I hate lying, but so often it just seems necessary. I tell him, "I fell off my bike. A guy got out of the car and grabbed the briefcase. A neighbor opened his door and yelled and the Mustang took off."

Dave stares at me, inviting more, but I keep my mouth shut. A hint of a grin starts and stops on his face and he shakes his head and starts eating again. With a fork full of potato and sour cream at his mouth he says, "Hamel."

"Not yet. I Googled the name of the geologist on the report. It turns out he and his brother both died in the last six weeks. I interviewed his widow and she thought Hamel did it. I did too, at the time. Then I went back to my friend's house and found him with a bullet in his chest."

"That would be Jimmy Ortiz."

"Yeah."

"He was your drug connection."

I was hoping to keep Jimmy on the sidelines, but it looks like Dave's ahead of me here.

"He's a friend of mine."

"Okay, but why did you go there and why would some-body shoot him?" Dave looks at me with that cop look, the one that says people have been bullshitting me all my cop life, and now you're spoon-feeding me some more.

"After the restaurant, I went to Jimmy's and stashed the papers in his bathroom. I think he got shot and they tossed his place looking for them."

"So that's when you got picked up and went to County."

"Yeah. Gotta love it there."

"Are we getting close to Hamel?"

"Coming right up. I get out of jail..."

Dave interrupts: "A free pass, no bail, charges dropped."

"Alan Hunter. He's part of this story."

Dave whistles. Cops don't like Alan Hunter; he's destroyed too many cases for them on technicalities.

"Tanya picks me up. I take her car and go to my house, but it's not there anymore. And Mindy's gone. My neigh-bor said you had stopped by."

"Semper Fi."

"That's him."

"So I follow the money and go to Jason Hamel's house. I'm there five minutes when the kid that took the briefcase shows up. I draw on him and ask where Mindy is. That's when the window shatters and a bullet hits Hamel."

"Who shot the bullet?"

"The kid's got a sidekick. Big dumb brute named Luke. I wing the kid in the shoulder and he bails. Now I get a story from Hamel while he bleeds out."

"You didn't call 911?"

"It wasn't happening, and he didn't want me to."

"So what's his story?"

"The kid is his adopted son, a pain-in-the-ass speed-freak who was directed to kidnap my daughter but decided to take her to Mexico because he was a psycho and thought he was going to marry her."

"Directed by whom?" I seem to have his interest now.

"I'm getting there. Hamel knows the kid killed the geologists, but he's only now coming around to admitting it. Anyway, he thinks the negative report on the mine investment is all wrong. He's convinced there's a huge deposit there, so he tries to quash the report so he can buy some time."

"Is that it?"

I shrug. "He died. The kid had a twenty-minute jump on me, but I knew where he was going. I followed him to the mine in Mexico and got Mindy back." There's not much point in telling him about Herbie and Melinda and their smuggling plan, or the Mexican gangbangers and their red devil tattoos, but Dave's going to make me squirm over Ratboy and Luke.

"You don't want to tell me how that went, do you?"

"Maybe another time?" The waiter is clearing our plates. Dave orders another drink and turns his attention back to me.

"Your story's an interesting one, but it isn't worth shit if it doesn't deliver me a perp. You promised I could close cases. So far, you owe me a dinner."

I don't have enough to pay for dinner, but I still have some story left. I tell him about Alan Hunter aiming me at the third party in this investment circus, Tanya's husband.

"Alan Hunter is the prime mover behind every piece of the puzzle, except for the kid being a wild card. I'm betting that by the end of the evening you'll be able to put the homicides and the kidnapping on Hunter. Fraud, too, if you can put it all together."

Dave looks at me suspiciously. His drink arrives and he treats it like a fat lady treats dessert. He signals the waiter for another and says to me, "What do you mean, by the end of this evening?"

"I still have to go somewhere, but I'll call you in the next hour or two and give you an address to meet me at. Do you have a pocket recorder?"

"Yeah, of course I do."

"Bring it."

"I'm never gonna find the kid and his partner, am I?"

"You might if you find a certain cave in the mountains near Ensenada."

Dave shakes his head and pulls out his wallet. The waiter brings his third drink and the bill. Dave slaps a credit card on the table and says to me, "So that's it?"

I say, "That's it for now." I don't like the look on his face.

He produces a manila envelope from the seat bench next to him and passes it to me. I undo the clasp and remove a glossy black-and-white photo. It's disturbing to look at, but fascinating, the blood caked in my hair, my eyes open, my teeth slightly showing.

Dave says, "That's a picture of a John Doe at the morgue. He disappeared in the middle of the night last Tuesday. Wednesday morning, actually."

I study the hole in my temple, touch the picture with my finger; I remember when my vision was black and white, and finally dull shades of gray.

"Charlie?"

I look up at Dave. His expression is almost sympathetic, but then it could be the Black Label. I'm at a loss for words.

"Maybe you had a twin brother you never told me about?"

I say, "Nope," and slide the picture back in the envelope. "Weird, huh?"

Chapter 34

I'm sitting in the Saturn, paralyzed. My hands are shaking and there's a muscle twitching where the bullet hole in my chest used to be, while a part of me watches calmly but can't intervene.

Too much has happened too fast and I haven't had time to digest the indigestible, to process the impossible and unacceptable fact of my experience.

I reach in my pocket and pull out my battered and nearly empty wallet. Daniel's card is barely readable. I dial the number.

After two rings a woman's recorded voice says, "Please enjoy the music while we locate the party you're calling," and I hear the Beatles singing, "Baby you're a rich man, baby you're a rich man..."

"Hello? Charlie, how dey be hangin'?"

"Cut the shtick, Daniel, I'm in trouble here."

"Tell me about it."

"I almost killed a man in a rage a few hours ago, I nearly broke down leaving my daughter, and now I'm frozen. I'm overwhelmed and I can't move." I watch Dave leave the restaurant and walk unsteadily to his car.

"It sounds to me as if you had a glitch in your repair job." He talks like he's describing a computer hardware problem.

"What kind of glitch?" I think back to my session in front of the mirror in the mine bunker, and the voice feeding me weird technical instructions.

"It has to do with the chemistry regulating emotions. Glutamate uptake transporters, that kind of thing. Once a strong feeling takes hold, it takes over and you don't have the mechanism to modulate it."

"What can I do about it?"

"Nothing right now. You'll need my help and some time in a safe environment."

"So why do you do this anyway? Follow me around and help me?"

"It's an obligation. I think it helps keep me alive. It'll be like that for you, too."

"Terrific. Now what?"

"Follow your plan. Depend on no one."

"That's it?"

"One thing. If you are gravely threatened, leave the body before it gets damaged."

Dave is fumbling with his keys. I don't have a good feeling about this.

¤ ¤ ¤

Tanya answers her door in a pale blue silk kimono. Her hair is loose, and without her boots she looks small and fragile. She has a drink in her hand and stands in my way as I try to walk in, her hand on my chest as she says, "Charlie, I'm so glad you called me."

I phoned her from the restaurant parking lot after signing off with Daniel, telling her I had her phone, did she want it? You bet she did.

She has music playing again, something exotic and slinky, a woman's smoky voice half singing, half talking in Portuguese. Scented candles barely illuminate the room and leave the edges in shadow. Tanya leads me by the hand as if we were on a dance floor, moving in time to the congas and acoustic bass coming from the speakers. She turns to me and lets the robe fall open. I place a hand on her breast and she moves in close. Her hair smells of fresh lemon with a hint of bergamot; I breathe it in and am transported. We dance in a cocoon of warmth and safety, there are no emergencies, there is no world outside of her scent and my hand on her breast and our slow movement and the voice singing *Eu te amo, estou enlouquecendo.* Desire floods my veins, more powerful than any drug I've known. From somewhere inside myself I watch and want to say *No, not now, not this,* but I'm only an observer and don't have a vote.

The sofa is covered with upholstery that's soft as velvet. Her skin, the fabric, my skin, the mix of fragrances, her slick wetness, my hunger, all become a hypnotic blend of sensation. Her beauty fascinates me; her body clings to me ferociously; we enter a timeless delirium where even my silent observer gets lost in the dream.

The music finally stops. A muscle in my leg twitches to its own rhythm. We lie drenched in sweat, staring at the moving shadows on the ceiling. Tanya rolls toward me and props herself up on an elbow. She runs a fingernail lightly across my chest.

I excuse myself and take my clothes to the bathroom. Jason Hamel's phone is in the left pocket of my jeans. I use it to text Dave: **Hamel house, gate/path from street, quiet, now.** I use Tanya's phone and find Alan Hunter's number, then text him: **Hamel house, the money, front yard, now.** I delete the record of the message and put on my clothes.

In the living room, I tell Tanya, "Get dressed. I have a surprise for you." She walks, stunningly naked in the half-light, to her bedroom.

¤ ¤ ¤

We take her car. The Oceana is on Ocean Avenue, the street that runs the length of Palisades Park, a strip of green that runs along the top of the cliffs overlooking the Pacific a hundred feet below. The north end of Ocean Avenue feeds down into Santa Monica Canyon. We arrive at Hamel's house in about three minutes. It's midnight, and I hope Dave is closer than Hunter.

Sitting in the BMW, I pull the key from the ignition and ponder the scene. The house is dark and protected from view from the street. I turn toward Tanya.

"Didn't you wonder why there were two reports with conflicting conclusions?" I still don't know how much she knew, and when.

"Alan told me that Jason faked the positive report so that he could buy time with the investors."

Something's rotten in Denmark, but I can't quite sniff it out.

Tanya follows me around the house to the place where I left the shovel. We walk to the front yard and I hand Herbie's flashlight to Tanya and point at the roses.

"Watch this."

Tanya watches in silence. I dig up the plants and set them aside. The flashlight illuminates the patch as it gets deeper.

Tanya says, "I'm sorry I got you into this."

I have no answer for her. The dirt piles up and I step into the recess as if into a shallow grave.

"Is your daughter okay?"

"Yes, thank you. My house has seen better days."

"I can help you with that if this is what I think it is…" She gestures with the beam of light.

"Money in the ground."

"Jason didn't trust the banks and he didn't trust cash. I should have figured this out."

"That's what private investigators are for." I look up and see that she's smiling.

I ask, "What are you going to do with it?" I feel the shovel hit the plywood cover.

"Cash out and run. Want to go with me, Charlie Miner?"

I dig out the dirt at the edges of the plywood and pull it out of the ground.

"I know a place in Puerto Vallarta. We could live there and travel. Bali, Majorca, Buenos Aires, we could do them all."

For some reason, the story of the frog and the scorpion occurs to me. I pull up the tarp and Tanya steps up to the edge of hole and plays the flashlight over the chests.

A burst of light floods my vision. I shield my eyes and look up to see Alan Hunter shining his own flashlight in my face. He's ten feet away. In his other hand is a gun with a silencer, also pointing at me.

"Well done, Charlie. I knew you'd come through in the end."

Alan Hunter is about five and a half feet tall, which puts him head to head with Tanya with her boots on. I squint down at him and wonder where Dave is.

"Actually, I had to connect the dots before I figured it out."

Hunter shifts his light to Tanya, who has turned around and is standing at the end of the hole, in front of the pile of uprooted rose bushes. She, too, shields her eyes, and says, "Alan, darling..."

He interrupts her and says, "Yes, Tanya, darling. Unpredictable as ever, but well done!"

She starts to step toward him, but now the silencer swings toward her and Hunter says, "No, Tanya, not this time. You stay where you are."

Tanya glances at me, confused, not in possession of all the information. For the first time since I met her, I see her unsure of herself, struggling for dominance at the wrong end of a gun. She says, "What are you going to do?" with a tremor in her voice.

"Tie up the loose ends and get back to the plan, Tanya. Everything was on track until you started meddling." He turns back to me. "Well, Charlie, how about you start piling those nice little chests over here?" He gestures with the light toward a spot on the path to the driveway. I pull the first chest out of the ground and place it on the path.

"So you had my daughter kidnapped and my house burned down."

"Yes to the first part. I needed the reports back. I already told you, the kid started the fire on his own. Then he went psycho on me and took off with your daughter. He said he wanted to marry her. Anyway, you caused all your own problems when you substituted copies for the real documents." He gestures, this time with the gun, at the hole. "Keep moving."

"I was looking out for my client. Something wasn't right; I just didn't know what it was." I pull another case out of the ground and look up at him. "And the dead geologists? What was that about?"

Hunter shakes his head and says, "You still don't get the whole picture, do you?"

I shrug and say, "I'm completely in the dark." I hope Dave's got my back, and that he's got a recorder on.

"Hasn't it occurred to you to wonder why there are two reports?"

"Yeah, it occurred to me. The positive one never made any sense. I thought maybe it was a forgery to show investors and keep them quiet." I pull out another case and put it on the ground.

Hunter bares his teeth, a hyena imitating George Clooney. "The negative report that Jason and Mickey wanted so badly to suppress is a fabrication. As managing partner, I was the first to hear the results of the report, which I assume you still have. It states that there are over six million ounces of gold at Santa Clarita, high grade and easily mineable. After expenses, that's probably a billion dollars. So I gave James a hundred thousand in cash and a promise of shares in the new company I was going to form if he would write an official report that the mine was a failure. He needed the money and took the deal."

"But he kept the original."

"We recovered it during his funeral."

Tanya's mouth is hanging open. She stamps her boot and says, "You miserable little prick. You were going to fuck all of us over!"

Hunter turns the gun back to Tanya. I watch her eyes go wide as Hunter says, "Lights out, baby," and shoots her in the forehead. The sound of the bullet striking bone and splashing into soft wet tissue is louder than the report from the muzzle. Tanya falls into the bed of thorns and roses. I stand, frozen, next to the hole, and wonder where Dave is.

Hunter swings the gun back my way and shoots me in the stomach. I fall backward on top of the remaining chests of gold and land splayed over them, my head propped against the edge of the hole. Hunter stands over me and shows teeth again.

"Ironic, isn't it?"

"What's that?" My nicely repaired body registers pain in a way I haven't experienced since I broke my back. It focuses me: Dave isn't here to help me; Daniel's voice is telling me *If you are gravely threatened, leave the body before it gets damaged.* But not yet. Hunter wants to gloat; he wants to tell his clever story.

"Ironic that we can have a nice conversation while you bleed out, just like you had with Jason."

"Yes, we should break out some cognac and have a toast to irony." I'm feeling light-headed. Like Jason's, my blood is seeping between my fingers as I hold my hand over the wound.

"When I called Jason and told him the bad news, he begged me to hold off on releasing the report. He wanted to use new money to drill more and show that the mine was feasible."

"So why kill the geologists?"

"The other brother, Mark, wouldn't cooperate. They argued and Mark was going to report what he knew to Jason and Mickey. When he died, James got cold feet and started threatening to talk, so we had to take care of that too."

I wish I had Jason Hamel's faith. The man had devoted his life to an idea I could never understand, but when his last moment came he was ready. I'm not.

"And the kid? Why did he do your dirty work?"

"His father talked Jesus at him until he wanted to pull the wings off flies. I taught him how to have fun. And his father gave him a few hundred here and there to do errands for him. I offered him ten thousand bucks to get me the reports by any means possible."

"Well, like you said, he sounds like a bit of a loose cannon." My voice is a pathetic croak. Fucking Dave.

"Yes he was."

"What do you mean, 'was'?"

"We've got a site manager down in Ensenada. He checks the mine property once every couple of weeks. He's got friends in the local police department, and boy did he have a story to tell. Dead bodies, explosions, and one crazy meth head jabbering about a guy looking for his daughter. But no Jason or Luke. Anyway, there's a loose end I'm guessing you tied up for me."

"And I'm your final loose end." I'm losing interest in this narcissist and his smug attitude.

"Not anymore." Hunter aims the gun at my forehead and starts to pull the trigger. I leave the body and rise into the night sky until Jason Hamel's house and yard are the size of a page in a book, and I watch pictures moving on the page as Alan Hunter's silenced gun twitches three times and my head snaps back and bounces forward as the bullets strike it. I rise farther until something seems ready to snap and I stop. Daniel's voice chimes in my head: *Commune with your spirit.* Ha! What else is there?

A miniature Alan Hunter far below me goes through my pockets, presumably looking for the geologist's reports. He pushes my body out of the way and begins to pull the remaining cases of gold out of the ground. There's movement from the other side of the house and I see Dave staggering up the path, his gun drawn. He nears the house and moves around it carefully until he is around the corner of the garage from where Hunter is scrounging in the hole.

Dave rounds the corner, gun pointing ahead of him. He stops. Hunter looks up. Do they exchange words? I don't know. Hunter's gun comes up, but not fast enough, and Dave fires. Hunter crumples into the hole that I had dug for him and Dave stands hunched over him, shoulders sagging, his gun at his side.

I hover, barely tethered. A shape approaches, an absence of light against the black sky, a triangle of darkness twice my size. I want to flee at top roaming speed, whatever that is, but once again I'm paralyzed. We're ten feet apart, drifting slightly toward each other; dread gives way to surrender and, like Jason Hamel, I am at last free of all resistance.

The shape seems to undulate slightly, a ripple that starts at its center and moves like a wave to its tips, and then it dives with astonishing speed. I follow more slowly and watch as it floats several feet over my body and then, with another ripple, moves to Tanya and descends and twitches in a voracious frenzy, like a shark feeding. It repeats its rape on Alan Hunter and ascends, blue streaks of electricity sparking in its darkness like lightning in a storm cloud. It ignores me and recedes into the sky. The roaring sound begins and grows until it engulfs me.

Time and space compress. In a vision from the sky, my silver strand to the world frayed and spider-web thin, I see thousands of junkies, hovering over the planet, superimposed as a second vision, looking down, lusting for another second chance at life.

. . . The End . . .

Acknowledgments

Lou Aronica, for going out on a limb with me; fellow writers Paul Simmons and Dave Putnam for keeping me on the path; and Chuck, Joe, Cliff, Borah, Michael—y'all know what for.

About the Author

Earl Javorsky is the black sheep of his family of artistic high achievers.